The Bucks of Goober Holler

The Bucks of Goober Holler

GILBERT MORRIS

Tyndale House Publishers, Inc.
Wheaton, Illinois

Originally published April 1985 as *Barney Buck and the Bucks of Goober Holler.*
Scripture quotations are from the *Holy Bible,* King James Version.

Library of Congress Cataloging-in-Publication Data

Morris, Gilbert.
The Bucks of Goober Holler / Gilbert Morris.
p. cm. — (Ozark adventures : 1)
Summary: Three brothers, due to be split up by the courts after the death of their parents, run off to the Ozarks to begin a new life together in an abandoned farmhouse.
ISBN 0-8423-4392-X
[1. Brothers—Fiction. 2. Orphans—Fiction. 3. Ozark Mountains—Fiction. 4. Christian life—Fiction.] I. Title. II. Series: Morris, Gilbert. Ozark adventures : 1.
PZ7.M8279Bu 1994 94-7012
[Fic]—dc20

Printed in the United States of America

99 98 97 96 95 94
7 6 5 4 3 2

To Lynn,
"Many daughters
have done virtuously,
but thou excellest
them all."

Contents

1
The Master Plan

IT was around the middle of March, and I was in algebra class, watching Mrs. Brown cover the board with *x*s and *z*s when Alice Gruber came in and made her announcement. "Note from the office for Barnabas." Holding it up, she looked across the room at me and waited as I slowly got up from my seat. I didn't even care when Ricky Potter whispered loud enough for everybody to hear, "Hey, Alice, you so struck by old Barney you gotta bring him love notes in class?"

While the class was giggling at that, and Alice sailed out with her nose in the air, I read the note: *Barney, Joe is sick again. I'm sending him home. Mr. Bartlett.*

That had made five times Joe had been sent home

since . . . well, since Mom and Dad had died in a car accident. I can say that now right out, but it took me a month to face up to it. I was going on thirteen and Joe was just a baby, only eight. Jake, our other brother, was ten. He was sort of tough and said that Joe would pull out of it. But he wouldn't eat and seemed to get paler every day.

I sat through algebra, then went to English, my next best subject. I was able to look alert even if my mind was off somewhere. I'd learned how to do that pretty well lately.

Jake was waiting for me after school, talking loudly with a couple of high school guys, and I had to pull him away. Jake looked the way Dad probably had at his age: short, chunky, with a big round head and straight black hair. Dad had always said Jake was a throwback to Great-grandma Buck, who was mostly Cherokee. When Jake got angry (which happened all the time), he could stare at you with those dark eyes of his, and it wasn't too hard to imagine him trying to scalp you. He was always getting himself into some crazy scheme that got him into trouble.

"Hey, Barney, let's go over to the new video game center with these guys, OK?" Those things fascinated Jake.

"We gotta go now, Jake," I said, and he finally fell in beside me. "Joe got sick again. And this is the day we're supposed to go with Miss Jean to see the judge."

"I don't like that old buzzard!" Jake frowned. "Why do we hafta go there?"

"Because we *do,* that's why." I took off walking as fast as I could. I was tall with long legs and Jake was short with short legs; so he couldn't get too far arguing with me.

Actually I was a little afraid of Judge Poindexter. Miss Jean—the lady the court had appointed to take care of us after the accident—said his bark was worse than his bite. But I'd rather get bitten once in a while than barked at all the time! Besides, I knew we couldn't go on forever as we had been. Ever since the funeral we'd been living in our house with Mrs. Futrell, the grouchy old woman who lived across the street—Mrs. Summers' mother.

I'd tried to tell Miss Jean that we could take care of ourselves, but she just shook her head. "It's required that you have adult supervision or go to Fairdale."

Fairdale. Just the word was enough to make you want to find the fastest exit and use it. Fairdale was the orphanage near Chicago. And I didn't care what it took, we weren't going to an orphanage! I mean, we might not have parents, but we still had each other. And no one was going to change that.

When Jake and I got to the house, Miss Jean's car was parked in front. Miss Jean was pretty old, maybe twenty-six. But she was so pretty I got tongue-tied every time we talked. She was blonde like Mom had been, with the bluest eyes and the longest eyelashes I'd ever seen.

When Jake first met her, he said right out, "Hey, you're a good-looking babe! You ought to be on TV instead of being a police lady!"

Her full name was Miss Jean Fletcher, and she wasn't a *real* police lady with a gun and all. She was an official in charge of kids in trouble and came by to check on us. All the time. Somehow I didn't think all the visits were official.

Miss Jean was standing up from the couch as we entered the living room; Joe got up, too. He'd been crying, and there was a damp spot on Miss Jean's shoulder. Of course, I didn't say anything because he was only eight.

"We have to hurry, boys," she said. "Our appointment with the judge is at four o'clock."

"Aren't you sick, Joe?" Jake asked. I knew he wanted to get out of the appointment, but it was no use.

"I . . . I guess I feel better now." Joe was as blond and fair as Jake was dark. He looked a lot like Mom. So Jake looked like Dad, and Joe looked like Mom. Nobody knew who I looked like. Dad used to rub my head and say, "Look at that mop of red hair! None of that in *my* family!" Then he would grin and say, "We really found you under a mulberry bush!" He could make red hair not seem so bad, though.

We all piled into Miss Jean's little Nissan and got to the Chicago Federal Building too fast to suit me. Judge Poindexter's office was a big, dark room on the second floor. He was waiting for us when we got there about five minutes late.

"You're late, Miss Fletcher!" he boomed. That's what he did. He didn't talk. He just boomed. He was a big man with lots of wild white hair and a sour face. He looked like a bulldog and growled like one, too.

He settled down behind his desk and picked up some papers. "Well, I don't think *this* will take long," he grunted. "Sit down! Sit down!"

Miss Jean nodded at us, and we all sat in the heavy oak chairs as she went to his desk. I could tell she wasn't a bit scared of him, and that made me feel better.

"You've seen the financial statements, Judge? And the Accounting Department's report?" she asked. I like the way she always got right to the point.

"Yes, and it's just as I've told you before, we don't have any choice in this case."

"I realize it's a difficult situation, Judge Poindexter, but there must be some way to—"

"You're new at this, Miss Fletcher," he interrupted with a wave of his big hand. "Every case has children involved, and most of the time they'll be in difficult positions. You'll just have to learn that the court has to do the best thing possible within those circumstances." He gave her a sour look and grunted. "You'll just have to throw your fairy-tale book away, Miss Fletcher. Life's not like that. Most people don't live happily ever after!"

"But at the very least, can't we wait until we can get them all in the same home?"

That was when it hit me. They were going to separate us! I glanced at Jake and saw he had that stubborn Indian look on his dark face. Joe's face was white as milk, and his lips were starting to tremble.

"That would be best, of course," the judge said, nodding, "but people in this area who are looking for foster children aren't looking for *three.* They usually want *one.* You must know that. And there are no relatives, isn't that correct?"

Miss Jean glanced at us. I would have swapped my chances of getting through the Pearly Gates right then for one measly half-uncle! But she shook her head. "We're looking for a cousin of Mrs. Buck's who is supposed to live in Ohio, and Mr. Buck may have distant relatives back in Arkansas. If you would just wait a few more weeks—"

"There's no time for that," the judge said impatiently. "The financial picture is so bad we need to start the process at once. Get the boys into places as soon as you can. Maybe the best thing we can hope for is that they'll be in the same city. They could visit from time to time."

He was talking about us as if we weren't there or

were deaf! It made me mad, and I suddenly didn't mind that Jake looked ready to scalp Judge Poindexter!

He'd made up his mind, though. "I want you boys to listen," he said, looking directly at us. "You've had a great misfortune. Losing both parents would be enough to unsettle anyone, and I must tell you that nobody can really help you with that. You'll have to learn to live and go on. Now, you've heard what I told Miss Fletcher. I wish we could keep you boys together, but it's not always possible to do what we'd like. You boys must make the most of it. You'll be placed in good homes—Miss Fletcher will see to that. And *you* see to it that you behave."

I guess he figured that was all we needed to hear. He just went back to the papers on his desk, and we all filed out. Miss Jean tried to make conversation on the way home, but none of us could say much. She probably saw how low we felt, because when we got to the house, she said, "I sure would like a Coke."

"We have some," I said. Everyone sat in the living room while I got Cokes ready and put some cookies on a tray. When I brought the refreshments out, she said, "How nice!" I knew she was trying to make things easier. But we all sat around feeling sort of stiff.

Finally Jake slammed his Coke down and said, "They're not gonna put *me* in any home!"

Then Joe started crying, and I said, "Miss Jean, there

must be *something* we can do! I mean for us to stay together."

She twisted her jacket sleeve and couldn't look any of us in the eye. "I don't know how to say this without making you feel sad, boys. The truth is that you're going to have to live in different homes." We pleaded with her for an hour, but I guess we all knew that nothing was going to help.

When she was ready to leave, I followed her outside. "Miss Jean, I . . . I really appreciate all the stuff you've done for us. I know it's not your fault the way things have worked out." Then taking me off guard, she grabbed me and held me tight. I was as tall as she was, but it felt kind of like it was my mom holding me. And even if I was the oldest, I have to admit it got to me! When she turned me loose and ran for her car, I swiped at my face with my sleeve.

When I got inside, Joe was watching TV as usual. It worried me the way that kid watched the tube hour after hour. He'd been pretty bad before Mom and Dad died, but since then he'd glued himself in front of the screen. Lately it seemed like the things he saw there were more real to him than the world around him. I didn't have the heart to say anything, though. What could I say?

Mrs. Futrell didn't have any trouble finding something to say, though. "That boy's eyes are gonna fuzz up and go out on him if'n he keeps starin' at that thing!" she muttered about a dozen times. I just nodded like I agreed and left the room.

Jake was in our bedroom staring at a poster of Arnold Schwarzenegger on the wall. I tried to talk to him, but he just grunted.

I fixed supper, but nobody ate much. That was another sign how down we were. When Mrs. Futrell first came to stay with us, she fixed us meals that would have killed a dog. The first time she set a plate in front of me, my eyes almost bugged out. The food looked and smelled strange—like it had been in the freezer for about a hundred years—and it tasted like two-ton cardboard. It wasn't long before Joe and Jake conned me into doing the cooking, and I had to admit that I'd actually gotten kind of good at it. So for Joe and Jake not to even touch a meal either meant Mrs. Futrell had cooked (which she hadn't) or they were too depressed to eat (which they were).

Mrs. Futrell was her usual cheerful self, too. "Never seen boys with such persnickety appetites," she muttered as we sat there. "Think you'd be glad to have good food in front of you."

Even though we all went to bed early to get away from Mrs. Futrell, none of us slept very well. We boys had all moved into the same bedroom. A couple of times I heard Joe making little noises, maybe because of a bad dream. Once I got up and noticed Jake was still awake, staring at the ceiling.

The next few days were pretty bad. I guess we were expecting somebody to come in and drag us off at any minute. Jake seemed to be thinking about something real hard, and Joe didn't move from the tube except to go to school. I got more and more depressed. It got harder and harder to act as if school and other things really meant something. The days were bad, but the nights were worse.

Sometimes Joe wasn't the only one having bad dreams.

But one thing bothered me almost more than anything else: Jake was hatching some scheme. He always was in one way or another, and he usually hooked me into it. And that usually meant a mess of trouble for yours truly. So I kept my eye on him, mainly because I thought he had running away from home on his mind.

I was wrong.

He sprang it on Joe and me about three o'clock Friday morning. I mean, not even the birds were awake yet!

"I've got it! Wake up, guys!" Jake was hollering and jumping up and down on the bed, waving some papers around. The lights were on, and I could see he had a wild grin on his face and a gleam in his black eyes. Joe woke up scared and tried to crawl under the covers. Jake ripped them off him and began shouting again, and we all fell off the bed.

"Cut it out, Jake!" I shouted. "Have you gone crazy?" I glanced at the door, just waiting for Mrs. Futrell to come storming in. Good thing she was hard of hearing!

"Yeah, I'm crazy!" He grinned, then tackled me, and we went down again. "I'm so crazy I've got a way to keep us all together! We'll show that old judge a thing or two!"

I finally pulled loose and stared at him. "What are you babbling about? I know you've been hatching something. What idiot scheme do you have now?"

"This!" He shoved a photograph at me, and Joe moved in to get a closer look. It was a picture of our grandparents. I'd seen it a thousand times.

"That's just Grandpa and Grandma," I said.

"No, it isn't," Jake said. "That's Uncle Roy Buck and his wife, Ellen. Why, Barney, I'm surprised you don't remember our uncle and aunt from Arkansas. The uncle and aunt who are going to take us and raise us!"

My brain was blank. What was he talking about? I looked at Joe, then back at Jake. But it only took seeing that wide grin of his before I realized what he was up to. "I see what's on your mind, Jake, and it's nutty as a pecan orchard." I grunted and looked at the picture again. "You've had a million wacky schemes, but this one is the *worst!*"

"Will you clam up? You haven't even *heard* the plan yet." Jake spread some papers on the bed and began his fast talk, which he did when he wanted to con me into something. "Look, maybe you forgot this stuff. See that house? Don't you remember about three years ago when Mom and Dad got all excited about the farm they inherited in Arkansas?"

"Sure, that was when Dad's uncle died," Joe said. "I remember that."

It came back to me then. "Yeah. We were gonna go live there someday, 'at the old home place,' Dad said. But what's that—"

"You dummy! All we have to do is convince the judge that Uncle Roy and Aunt Ellen want us to come and live with them. Then we can go there and we won't be split up. Can't you see that?"

"I can think of about a hundred reasons why it *won't* work! In the first place, they're gonna sell this house and any other property the folks had. But even if they would let us go, people are living in that house. I heard Dad say so. And if that wasn't so, we still couldn't fool the whole town into thinking we had parents."

"I have that all worked out," Jake said. "What do you think I've been working on the last few days? Look." He held up a letter and shoved it under my nose. "In the first place, the renters moved out about a year ago. Here's a letter from the people that handled it. And they said it's too far out to rent anymore. And nobody's gonna sell it, because nobody knows the folks had it."

"How could that be?" I asked.

"I guess nobody found the drawer where Mom kept all that stuff." That wasn't too surprising. Mom had this special drawer in her desk. It was kind of a hidden drawer behind another drawer, and you had to know where to look to find it. She kept all her "important papers" in there. I'd forgotten all about it.

Jake just went on. "Well, the deed was there with the pictures. So the judge and Miss Jean know about *this* house, but *not* the one in Arkansas." Jake grinned. "And who's gonna tell 'em?"

"But they would never fall for it, Jake. Not in a million years. Courts have to have proof!"

"So here's the proof," Jake said, holding up another sheet of paper. "It's a letter from Uncle Roy and Aunt Ellen saying that they've been away on vacation and just heard that Mom and Dad passed away. *And* how much they want us to come and live with them."

I read the letter, and it was so convincing I almost believed it myself. Jake had used just the right kind of writing for people from the South.

"But it wouldn't be honest to use this, Jake," I argued. "Besides, we might get put in jail for it. Anyway, we've never lived on a farm. How in the world do you think we could take care of ourselves in the country?"

Jake scrunched his face up and said, "OK, so it isn't exactly honest. You wanna be honest and get split up, or do you wanna do something to keep us together? This Sunday school stuff is all right for some things, but you gotta have a little common sense! As for living in the woods, I guess we can learn as we go, can't we?"

All at once I felt Joe pulling at me. I looked down at him and noticed his eyes were alive and shining in a way I hadn't seen them in a long time. I opened my mouth to tell him the plan was impossible, but I just couldn't. I was the oldest, and it was up to me to do something. Nutty as Jake's idea was, it was better than losing each other!

I straightened my shoulders. "All right, Jake, tell us the rest of it."

He had it planned out up to a point. After we'd gone around and around it for about an hour, I finally said, "Jake, maybe we can pull the wool over that judge's eyes, and maybe we can fool Miss Jean, but we'll never in this world convince those people in Arkansas that we're a family with parents and everything."

Jake narrowed his eyes, deep in thought. "How about if you dress up like a grown man, Barney, and play like you're our dad?"

"Sure, you could do that, Barney!" Joe piped up, his eyes bright.

I shook my head. "It would never work, not in a

million years. How could a kid like me convince—" Then all of a sudden I stopped short. An idea had just hit me like a bolt of lightning. "Unless, of course, we could . . ."

"We could *what?*" Jake demanded. "You got an idea, don'tcha, Barney?"

"Well, maybe I got a piece of one," I said slowly, thinking hard. "Look, I'm not even gonna tell you about it until I see if it'll work. Now we gotta keep quiet about all this, you know?"

Jake and Joe both promised, and we got up, dressed, and had breakfast. When we got to school, I said, "Jake, you be sure to meet Joe after school today. I have something to take care of." Jake tried to pry it out of me, but I walked off and left him.

As soon as school was out, I hightailed it over to Clyde Rodger's place, about five blocks from our house. I didn't want Jake and Joe to know what I was up to, so I darted around some side streets and got there just in time. Clyde was backing out of his driveway in his pickup truck, and I almost got run over trying to stop him.

"Hey!" he yelled when he stopped and pulled the truck back onto the driveway. "You gone crazy, Barney? I could've run right over you!"

"I gotta talk to you, Clyde! Right now!" He jumped down from the truck and started to argue, but I caught him by the arm and pulled him back toward his house. When we got inside, I got right to the point. "Clyde, you've *got* to help us—me and Jake and Joe."

Clyde's round face was always ready to break into a grin. He gave me his biggest smile and said, *"Anything,* Barney. You name it, and it's done. That's what I promised your dad."

Clyde had been Dad's best friend. They'd been in the army together and had worked at the same steel mill for a long time. Before Clyde and his wife, Ruby, got divorced, they were at our house all the time, and we felt at home at their house just as much as we were at our own. After the divorce, Clyde bought an old house with a double carport and quit his job to go on the road to catch auctions all over the country—mostly in the South and East. When his truck was full of old furniture and things, he would come back to sell the stuff. We didn't see him as much then.

After the funeral, he took me aside and said, "Barney, I wanna tell you about something I promised your dad. We were talking one time about what to do if something *happened* to him, you know? I told him if anything ever happened to him, I'd see to it that you kids were taken care of. And I mean to do just that."

Since our parents had been killed, he hadn't missed many chances to spend time with us. Although he was gone a lot, he'd really made things a lot easier for us.

He would stick around for a while, then pile into his truck and head out for auctions. He'd turned his old house into an antique shop—a junk store would be closer to it. I knew he missed his wife, and Jake and I kinda figured he was just traveling around trying not to be lonesome. He was short and getting fat from eating so much junk food.

So now Clyde was nodding and repeating, "Anything I can do, Barney."

I knew he meant it. "Clyde keeps his word." That's what my dad had always said.

"Clyde, they're gonna split us up. Judge Poindexter said so! You gotta help us!"

"But, couldn't Miss Jean—"

"No. She can't do anything except what the judge says. But we got a plan, Clyde. Only it won't work without you. If you'll help us, we can stay together!"

"Shoot, Barney," Clyde said, leaning back in a kitchen chair.

I told him the whole thing—how we'd made up these relatives and were going to try to convince the judge and Miss Jean that they were ready to adopt us. "What we need, Clyde, is for you to go with us to Arkansas and act like you're our dad, you know? I mean, you wouldn't have to *stay* or anything like that. Just go to the school and to the stores—you know, establish your identity." With any other adult I would've felt like a fool even saying such stuff, but Clyde was so much like a kid himself that it wasn't hard to get right at him.

"What about when I leave?" he asked.

"Then we'll say you're off on a business trip. And you have to go pretty close to Arkansas all the time, don't you? Couldn't you just drop in when you're close?"

Clyde's brow got all wrinkled for a few minutes, and I figured he was thinking real hard. Then he sat up and banged his hand on the table. "Shoot! I'll do it!"

I almost hollered I was so relieved. But I didn't. Instead, I thought I'd better try to point out that it might get a little sticky—like if the judge found out what we were up to!

Clyde grinned like a kid with a new toy. "Son, you're talking to a man who once crawled across Vietnam with nothing but an M-1 and nerve! Why—"

I'd heard his war stories before, so I broke in. "But about Miss Jean, if you'll offer to *take* us to Cedarville, I think she'll be more likely to go for it."

He said, "Son, women have *never* given me trouble!"

I knew that wasn't so, but I didn't argue with him.

Well, that's how the Master Plan got started.

Somehow, Jake got a letter mailed from Cedarville from our "relatives" and got Miss Jean to agree that we should go stay with them. 'Course, she would never have agreed if it hadn't been for Clyde. He went to see her and said that he had to go right through Cedarville,

and he could take us right there. He even agreed to meet our uncle and aunt and bring her back a report.

That settled it. Miss Jean started on the paperwork, and we had to meet with the judge. We all kept quiet and tried to look excited about our long-lost relatives showing up. And I almost hollered again when the judge said it would be all right for us to make a "trial visit" to Arkansas.

In less than two weeks we were sitting in the cab of Clyde's bob truck with all our stuff in the back.

Mrs. Futrell and Miss Jean were there to say good-bye.

"I baked you boys some cookies for your trip," Mrs. Futrell said, handing me a lunch bag that weighed a ton. I wondered what she'd put in the cookies to make them weigh so much. Then I felt I should be more grateful.

"Thanks, Mrs. Futrell. We'll think about you when we're eating them." I gave the bag to Joe for safekeeping. Maybe Mrs. Futrell wasn't so bad after all.

Miss Jean had a big grocery bag filled with all kinds of stuff: peanuts, crackers, apples, Coke, and cookies. "Here, boys. Maybe this will keep you a little occupied on your long trip. Don't forget to write me!" She looked kind of sad, like maybe it was pretty hard for her to be sending three kids off on an eight-hundred-mile trip to the backwoods.

I wondered what she would have looked like if she'd known the *truth!*

"Good-bye, Barney," she said, trying to smile but not doing real well. "Good-bye, Jake. Good-bye, Joe. You take your vitamins and watch out for snakes! And . . ." Miss Jean looked real worried.

I had a sinking feeling when I looked out the window and saw her face. She really loved all of us. And we'd lied to her like anything! Somehow I knew, as Clyde pulled out and we watched her fade into the distance, that all the lies we'd told and all the shortcuts we'd taken—no matter *how* important they'd seemed to be—were gonna catch up with us sooner or later!

2

The Old Home Place

AT first the trip was fun. Jake, Joe, and I had never traveled much, and Clyde had been over the road so much he knew lots of stuff to point out. But it got old pretty fast. Five hours later we were miserable—bored and uncomfortable, all scrunched up on the hard, narrow seat.

Once we tried to get in the back and lie down, but it was dark and there was no rug or blanket to lie on. Finally we gave up and slept the best we could huddled together in the cab.

It rained for the last four hours of our trip. I was dozing with the side of my head smashed against the glass when Jake said, "Wake up, Barney. We're here!"

I stared out the window, but it was cloudy and the rain was still coming down. All I could see was the Cedarville bus station. Clyde jumped out and began opening the tailgate of the truck. The rest of us jumped out and watched him unload our stuff.

"Look," he said quickly, "I wish I had time to help you guys find the place, but like I told you, the auction at Shreveport starts early and I'll have to drive hard to get there. You think you can make out? Find a cab and get there?"

I stared at the grubby little bus station. "Well, sure, Clyde."

"Great! Now, I'll be back soon as I can. Tomorrow, maybe. I'll find your place and we'll get the old Master Plan off the ground. All right?"

It had to be all right, because, as soon as he helped us get the stuff out of the rain, he roared off, leaving us all alone. I felt a little bit like Robinson Crusoe must have felt when he was left all alone on the beach. There we were, stranded in a strange place with all our baggage in a big pile, and we didn't know a soul. We were at the end of a street with lots of business places, but all of them looked closed.

"Well, we sure didn't get a brass band to greet us, did we?" I said. "Let's ask if we can get a ride to the house."

On the trip to Cedarville, we'd been inside a few small-town bus stations to buy candy and pop. This one was just as dreary and run-down as the rest. There was a counter with an old man sitting behind it, a Coke machine that said Out of Order, four cane-bottomed chairs, a vending machine with some sad-looking potato chips, and a funny-looking dog with one blue eye and one brown eye.

"Say, mister," I said to the old man, "can you tell us how to get a taxi?"

He peered at us, spit in a coffee can that was too close to my hand, and said, "Pretty late. Taxi driver's probably gone off duty."

"Gee, we sure do need a ride. Could you call him?"

"Guess I can do that. Cost you extra if he has to come back from his place."

"That's all right."

The Wonder Bread clock over his head said it was only 4:15, but at this time of the year it got dark early. Besides, big black clouds were piling up and it looked ready to let loose with a downpour. We all listened while the old man talked on the phone to somebody named Charley. He argued with him for some time, then hung up and said, "Charley said he'd come soon as he finished his banana pudding. Couldn't do better'n that, could he now?"

"Thanks a lot." We went outside and waited for fifteen minutes. Then an old blue Buick pulled up. The windshield had a hand-painted sign that said Taxi.

A skinny old man got out. "All right, all right, you gonna stand there all night? These all yours? Have to charge you extra. . . ." The man rattled on nonstop, but we helped him load the trunk and then got in. "By the way, folks around here call me Charley. You can do the same. Now where you wanna go?"

Jake had gotten a map as part of the Master Plan, so he whipped it out and pointed at a spot. "Right *there.*"

Charley glared at us, then began pointing at the map and muttering. "Let's see. There's the Interstate and there's the *Y*. . . . Must be the old farm road—" Then he stopped and looked up in surprise. "Why, this here is the old Buck place!"

"That's right," I said. "You know where it is?"

That must've insulted him. "You think I'm some whippersnapper just moved into town?" he piped up. "Why you wanna go there for?"

Joe started to answer, but Jake gave him a sharp nudge and said, "We better get started. Looks like rain."

Charley snapped his jaws shut, started the old car, and headed out without another word. I tried to see the way we were going since I was going to have to come into Cedarville the next day, but I got mixed up with the turns he took. As we went down several streets, I noticed Cedarville looked like a pretty nice place—what I could see of it, anyway—lots of nice clean houses with neat yards and big trees overhanging the wide streets.

Finally we turned off on a broad highway and headed west. Charley suddenly tried his best to pump us, but we all kept our mouths shut. After about ten minutes I began getting worried.

"I don't see any houses," I said. "Is this still Cedarville?"

"You want the old Buck place?"

"Sure."

"The old Buck place ain't in Cedarville."

"What! Where *is* it?" I asked, feeling more uneasy.

"It's in Goober Holler."

"Goober Holler!" The name sounded terrible! "What's Goober Holler?"

"Used to be a town. Ain't *nothing* now. Old man Simmons owns most of the land. All of it 'cept the Buck place." Charley paused long enough to give us time to tell who we were, but we didn't oblige. He snorted and pulled off the road with a jerk of the wheel. "You'll have to walk from here."

We piled out and looked down a sorry-looking road that was almost hidden by overgrown trees and knee-high weeds. "We can't walk down *that!"* I said.

"Will if you have to," Charley snapped. "Look at that mud! My cab wouldn't get ten feet in it. Get stuck for sure. Take a four-wheel drive to git through that mess!"

"But—how far is it to the house?" Jake asked.

"'Bout a quarter mile I 'spect. I useta hunt birds

there, but it's been a long spell. You better git started. Looks like it might rain pretty good."

He was out and had the trunk open before we could think of anything else to say. "That'll be five bucks." He took the money I gave him and seemed to soften a little. "That's higher than usual, but I had to leave my banana pudding, you see. Well, you boys better git moving!" He hopped into the old car and wheeled around in a U-turn, splattering us with mud. Then he disappeared down the highway.

We stood there looking pretty sad. Jake was peering into the dark woods, and Joe was moving in close to me. I didn't feel too cheerful myself, but I was the oldest, so I did my imitation of Oliver Hardy. I looked at Jake and said, "Well! Here's another fine mess you've gotten us into!"

Jake didn't even know I was trying to be cheerful. He looked down the muddy road and said, "I don't like the looks of this."

I gave my best don't-worry-I've-got-it-all-under-control laugh and picked up one of the suitcases. "Let's go, you guys. You wanted adventure, didn't you? Since we can't carry all these suitcases, let's just put them behind that tree. We'll get 'em tomorrow."

Jake took a big suitcase, I took a bigger one, and Joe clung to one of the little ones. I waded into the weeds, and they followed. As soon as we started down the road, it got darker. The trees cut off what little light was left, and the mud sucking our feet at every step didn't help. All of us were huffing after a few minutes, and it got even darker.

"Are—are there wolves out here, Jake?" Joe asked in a very small voice.

"Of course there aren't wolves!" I answered.

Just then a wolf howled.

It was really a coyote. They're so shy you practically never see one, but we didn't know the difference until later.

"Probably a lost dog," I said feebly. "Let's hurry up, huh?"

Finally Jake said, "There it is!"

We stared through the dark at the shadowy outline of a white house. Moving closer, we saw that it was just an old wooden house with a big fireplace on the side and a screened-in porch all the way across the front. The windows were mostly broken out, and the gate of the fence was hanging by one hinge.

"Looks like a place Frankenstein might live in," Jake said gloomily. "Or Dracula."

"Well, that's a cheerful thought!" I snapped at him. "Look, let's get inside and get a fire going. There's some wood stacked on the porch."

I reached through one of the broken windows and unlocked it, then we crawled through. I was glad I had bought one of those throwaway plastic flashlights—the kind you squeeze and the light comes on. I ran its little gleam across the room. There was some furniture, but it seemed mostly broken down. I didn't really care, though. The fireplace was what we needed right away.

"Get some of that dry wood in. It's gonna be plenty cold tonight—and this flashlight won't last forever."

I guess the thought of being in the dark inspired us, because we had a fire going pretty quick. We hauled in lots of the dry wood.

A north wind made the trees near the house scratch at the windows, and if you glanced up at just the right time, it looked as if the branches were skeletons trying to get in. So I just didn't glance up. The fire popped, and there was a creaking in the attic. The fire was warm, but it made weird shadows on the wall. No matter how I tried to talk myself out of thinking it, I realized this was about the creepiest, spookiest place I'd been in for a long time. And I'd brought my brothers here to live.

I don't mind saying I felt about as low as I ever did—except when we had lost our parents.

Jake and Joe weren't too thrilled, either. Jake, tough as he was, was pretty quiet. He kept moving closer to me, and Joe was holding on to him.

I gave myself a shake and made myself sound cheerful.

"Well, here we are, in good ol' Goober Holler. Isn't

that *something!"* Then the wind gave a spiteful howl, which made me shout right back: "Go on! Holler all you want to! The Bucks are here and we aim to stay!"

Jake and Joe laughed at that, and I went right on. "We'll get the suitcases tomorrow, but tonight we have *this!"* I'd brought along the food Miss Jean had packed. We'd already eaten the sandwiches, but the fruit and canned goods were in good condition. I'd added a lot of stuff, too, from the bus stations we'd stopped at—like potato chips, soda, and oatmeal cookies.

"Let's fix us something to eat, all right?" I jumped up and asked Jake to find something to heat water in. Joe helped me unpack our stuff. "Let's have our first picnic . . . in our own place!" I exclaimed.

That night we really outdid ourselves. Jake found some old pans, and we heated some soup in the fireplace. We made some cocoa and floated marshmallows in it. We had Snickers bars, potato chips, peanuts, pecans, Cheez-Its, and a bunch of other junk food. We just pitched in and actually got to laughing and having a good time!

I was pretty pleased with myself. After I got Jake and Joe all bundled up in their heaviest clothes, I built up a big fire and made bedrolls out of some clothes. I made Joe say his prayers, and even Jake mumbled a little bit.

Jake and Joe were so played out, they dropped off to sleep right away, but I didn't. I dozed on and off, but I never really slept—maybe because I knew I had to get up to throw logs on the fire when it burned down. I was also thinking about the next day. *I'm the oldest, and I'm going to have to handle all the mean jobs. Yuk!*

Finally I went to sleep, but the last thing I remembered was something that had happened a long time ago when we were all little kids. It was when I was eight and had talked Dad into letting the three of us sleep in our tent in the backyard. That was a big deal then. Just before Dad had left for the night, he'd stuck his head inside the tent and said, "Barney, you're the oldest. Look out for Jake and Joe."

During the night I must've dreamed about that, because I remember waking up and mumbling to myself, "I will, Dad! I'll look out for them!"

3
Mr. Buck Goes to Town

WE spent the next morning sleeping. I guess the trip had caught up with us. It was nearly one o'clock in the afternoon by the time we all got up. We'd pigged out the night before, so there wasn't that much to eat. The inside of the house looked a lot worse by the cold light of day. Still, we made do.

Clyde came in about eight o'clock that night with a bunch of fried chicken from Colonel Sanders and a couple bags of groceries. We built up the fire and stayed up until about eleven making plans.

Around eight o'clock the next morning, Clyde and I left for town. "You guys, don't wander off, you hear?" I hollered out the car window to Jake and Joe.

"They'll be all right," Clyde said with a grin. "I figure if a burglar comes, Jake'll take him for all he's got. I guess all this was his scheme, right?"

"Yeah, most of it. And I admit, Clyde, that I've had some second thoughts about the whole thing."

"You scared?"

"No, not really."

"Well, what is it then?"

It was hard to explain, but I had to talk it out with somebody. "There's one thing that bothers me about this whole business, and that's the way we've gone about it. I mean, look at what we've had to do—forge letters, lie, and fool Miss Jean. And there's a lot more of that stuff ahead if we stay here."

"You don't have much choice, do you?" Clyde asked, swerving to miss a dead possum. He gave me a funny look. "Look, wouldn't your folks want you guys to stay together?"

"They wouldn't want us telling *lies!*" I said. "You know how both of them felt about that."

"Sure, I know. If there were ever two Christians in this world, it was your folks." He was quiet for a while. I could tell he was concentrating. Then he said, "You gonna go back, Barney? I mean, if you feel it's wrong and all . . ."

I didn't answer him. I didn't know what to say! I wanted to tell him to take me back to the home place, but then what? I knew Mom and Dad would have wanted us to be a family, to stay together. I also knew they wouldn't like what we were doing. Finally, I shook my head. "No. Let's go on with it, but I wish there was another way, Clyde. I really do."

Neither of us said much, and Clyde stopped at a gas station to find out where the school was. He found it without any trouble—a big red-brick building just off the highway with a bunch of kids milling around outside. We got out of the truck, and I followed Clyde as he bulldozed his way through the crowd and pushed open the big glass doors.

"There's the principal's office," I said. We entered a room and were greeted by a blue-haired lady behind a tall counter.

"May I help you? I'm Mrs. Taylor," she said.

"Like to see the man in charge," Clyde replied.

"That's Mr. Moore." Mrs. Taylor walked to a door with a frosted glass window and looked inside. "Mr. Moore, there's a gentleman to see you."

After a few seconds, she said, "Go right in."

A fat man with a little fringe of hair around his ears was sitting behind a walnut desk that was littered with papers. He got up and introduced himself. "Good morning. I'm Vincent Moore."

Clyde took his hand and said in a loud southern-style voice, "Howdy, my name's Buck, and this here's my boy

Barney." He was trying to talk like a character on "Hee Haw." Actually I thought he was overdoing it a little, but Mr. Moore just nodded. "Jest moving in, neighbor, from Illinois. Be stayin' out to Goober Holler. So I want my three boys to get enrolled in your school."

"Well, that's fine, Mr. Buck," Mr. Moore said. "I hope you enjoy our little community."

"Here's their report cards and the other stuff the school people gave me to pass on to you." He handed Mr. Moore our reports and then gave me a hard look. "I just wanna say, Mr. Moore, if any one of my young'uns gives you any trouble, beat the tar outta him! That's my policy, sir, and I'm tellin' you to do the same."

Mr. Moore looked a little surprised. "Well, well, we don't—that is to say, we find it unwise—as a *rule,* that is—to use corporal punishment."

Clyde was into his act now. He slapped his hand against his thigh and said at the top of his lungs, "Whup the fire outta any one of 'em!"

"Yes, well—we'll have to see—"

"And another thing, don't be botherin' to come at me with PTA and other kinds of stuff! You take charge of the learning, and I'll take care of the home business. Miz Buck and me, we don't *visit!* And my boys gonna have plenty to do without messin' around with a bunch of school extree-curricular mess. You understand?"

Mr. Moore looked a little stunned. The louder Clyde

spoke, the softer his voice got. "Yes, I believe I catch your meaning."

"You wanna tell me something, you tell it to my boy Barney." He slapped me on the back so hard I almost collapsed. Then he went on, "We ain't sociable, Mr. Moore. So, you jest tell Barney, and he'll tell me. And I'll either call or write a note, but I wouldn't come callin' if I was you, you understand?"

"Yes, I suppose so," Mr. Moore said, clearing his throat.

"That's good! Well, you take care of the learnin'—and I'll take care of the rest at home!" Clyde grabbed me by the arm and hauled me out into the hallway just as the bell rang. We met the rush of kids on their way to class, but Clyde just plowed right through, towing me along with him.

When we were back in the truck, he laughed. "How was that, Barney?"

"Good! I don't think you can count on Mr. Moore making a pest of himself out at the place. You think you can be as nasty as that to a few more people?"

"Shoot, yeah!" He grinned. "Where next?"

"The gas company. I saw it on the highway back before we turned in to the school." I directed him, and we found the place without any trouble. "That's it, the Ace Propane Company."

We got out and entered the building. A young guy in

the office smiled when we went in, but Clyde made himself so obnoxious by the time we left that he had a frown on his face. He agreed to send a truck out and fill up the tank and looked real relieved when we left. When we got back in the truck, Clyde said, *"That* ought to get the word around about the Bucks."

"I guess so," I said with a smile. "If you can keep it up, we'll have such a reputation for being cantankerous nobody will *dare* set foot on the Buck place!"

We'd figured making everyone think the Bucks were about as unfriendly as a cornered bobcat was the best way to keep people away from us. And we hoped nobody would think much of the fact that Clyde wasn't seen much.

We worked like beavers all morning. We picked up a bunch of groceries at the Piggly Wiggly supermarket. Next we went to the post office and got a box in the name of Roy Buck and told the lady in charge who we were and to hold any mail that came for us. She looked like a gossipy type; so I decided it was like putting an announcement in the paper that the Bucks were moving in. We went to the electric company and put down a deposit, then to the hardware store and got a bunch of stuff—pots, pans, tableware, a can opener, and stuff like that. Afterwards, we went by the bank and opened a checking account in the name of Roy Buck.

Was that scary! "Clyde, can't I go to jail for that?"

"For what?" he asked with a grin. "You're Roy Barnabas Buck, ain't you?"

"Sure, but they think I'm *you!* I mean, they don't know that I'm *me."*

"Now don't get all tangled up," Clyde said soothingly. "It's your money, Barney, and if we gotta do this to get at it, why that's all there is to it."

"I guess so, but it doesn't seem right."

At noon we stopped for hamburgers and shakes. That was when I called Miss Jean. She'd told me to call collect, and I'd promised her I would, but it wasn't any fun.

"Miss Jean? This is Barney."

She sounded so good it made me want to see her. Then I had to start telling about twenty-five lies a minute, with gusts up to fifty! We were fine . . . Uncle Roy and Aunt Ellen were *real* nice . . . things couldn't be better—stuff like that. I didn't give Miss Jean time to ask many questions, but I did tell her there wasn't a phone at the house. I gave her our new post office box number and promised to write soon. I even promised I would have Uncle Roy write.

"Barney, I'm so *happy* for you!" she finally said. "It's wonderful the way things have happened, isn't it? I think the Lord must be looking after you!"

I had to bite my tongue to keep from blurting out the truth!

I knew Miss Jean was a Christian, like Mom and Dad had been. Like I was supposed to be. It was like getting hit with a hammer to have her say that about God helping us. All I could think of was how many wrong things we'd done to get this far. Now to have her talk like that made me mumble something and tell her I would call back later. Then I hung up.

Clyde was waiting for me in the truck. "You told her everything was all right?"

I waited until he had pulled out on the road and was headed for Goober Holler until I answered. "That's what I told her."

He probably could tell I was worried, so he didn't say anything. When we got back to the house, Jake and Joe were ready to hear all about it.

As we unloaded the stuff, Clyde said to all of us, "I'm proud of you guys. I mean it." He was serious for once, and I knew he was a little bit worried about leaving us alone. "Lots of families are breaking up, you know? And I wouldn't want that to happen to you."

I knew he was thinking about his own home. "Don't worry, Clyde. We'll make it, and you can take all the credit. We couldn't have done it if you hadn't helped us."

Clyde looked around as Joe and Jake pulled at him and said thanks, and I could swear his eyes grew a little misty. "Well, I promised your dad, you know," he said.

"Say, what did you guys do all day while we were gone?" I said to change the subject.

Jake and Joe gave each other a look. Something was up. "Well, for one thing we've been kind of exploring," Jake said, giving Clyde and me a funny look. "Somebody's been around this place a lot. Matter of fact, somebody's been living here."

"What! In *our* house?" It was funny how soon we'd become possessive about the place! "How do you know?"

"There's some trash—soup cans and stuff like that. And it's pretty new-looking. I think somebody's been eating around here."

"Probably a bunch of kids," I said. "Wouldn't we do it ourselves if we found a vacant house we could get into? Someone was probably using it for a clubhouse."

Jake and Joe looked at each other again, and Jake shook his head. "This is no kid. Come and see."

All of us went into an upstairs bedroom. Jake pointed to a cot with a dirty old mattress, and a dirty blanket for a sheet. Whoever had been using the cot must've been pretty tall. I judged about six feet, from the length of the outline his body had left on the bed.

"Probably a bum or a tramp," Clyde said. I could tell he was trying not to show his concern.

"He's a big one," Jake said. "What do we do if he comes back?"

"Why, I guess we'll tell him the Bucks of Goober Holler are back to stay. He'll just have to find another place."

"I saw some guns for sale at the hardware store," Clyde said. "Why don't I pick one up right away? I need to pick up some window glass anyway."

Jake looked at the cot again and nodded. "He may have a friend. Better get two guns."

"And a pellet gun for me!" Joe added.

Clyde left for town right away. When he got back, he had a shotgun for me, a .22 caliber rifle for Jake, and a pellet gun for Joe.

Somehow we all felt a little strange holding those weapons. Back in Chicago, Mom and Dad had always told us to be careful because of muggings and all, but they'd never kept a gun in the house.

Clyde spent an hour or two outside fixing some windows and then showed us how to use our guns and take care of them. "You don't use these unless you really need to, you hear? And think twice about using them even if you think you need to!" He seemed nervous about leaving us this time, especially with the guns.

I wasn't all that calm, either, but what could we do? We Bucks needed some protection, being without parents and all.

"You boys take care of yourselves. I'll be back in ten days, but you call me if you get into a jam," Clyde said, getting into the truck. We watched it rumble down the narrow road. Then we went back into the house. We began cleaning up the dishes, and I described what Clyde and I had accomplished in town.

Suddenly Jake punched my arm. "You son of a gun!" he said.

I wasn't very good at most things. I couldn't play ball very well, and Jake made better grades than I did. I was clumsy and couldn't make things with my hands like Joe. I couldn't sing or do anything artistic. I knew Jake and Joe loved me because I was their brother, but I'd never done much they could admire. Now I had, and it felt pretty good!

Jake punched my arm again and said, "Yeah, Barney! Nobody could've done that but *you!*"

Joe's eyes were shining. It was too soon to boast—things could still fall apart—so I just said, "Well, it didn't go bad, but we still have a long way to go."

Just how long a way, we would soon find out.

4

New Boys at School

THE next morning, the three of us stood beside the road, shivering from the March frost. A big school bus, packed out with kids, came around the bend and stopped for us. I'd made sure we looked OK, but we still got funny looks, and some of the kids whispered something about us. New kids always get stares.

After about ten more stops we pulled onto the school grounds. I led the way to the office. Mrs. Taylor stared at me so long when I told her our names that I thought she recognized me. It turned out that she was just real nearsighted. She gave me three sheets of paper and said, "Here are your schedules. Do you want someone to take you to the right rooms?"

"No, ma'am, but maybe I'd better go with Joe here the first time." We left the office, and I handed Jake and Joe their schedule sheets. "Can you find your way, Jake?" I asked.

He nodded. "Sure. See you after school." He was off, and I noticed that he was talking to some kid before he got out of sight. Jake could meet people in the middle of the Sahara, I guess, but Joe and I had a little more trouble.

Joe's room was in a different building, which looked like a line of metal classrooms that must have been tacked on for more room. "This is it, Joe," I said when we got to Room 104. "Let me do the talking."

When we went in, a middle-aged woman looked up from her desk. I was glad to see she had a kind-looking face. "I'm Barney Buck, Mrs. Green, and this is my brother Joe. He's supposed to be in your class."

Joe handed her his schedule sheet, and she smiled at us. "Well, that's fine, Joe. You want to put your things over there?"

"Mrs. Green, can I talk to you outside for just one minute?" I asked.

"Why, of course." She gave the class a steely glance aimed to keep them still, then followed me outside.

"Well, it's like this, Mrs. Green," I said nervously. "Joe is real smart in lots of ways, but he's got a problem.

You see, the doctors said he can't see words right. It's like he sees them backwards, they say. So he can't read."

"Oh." Mrs. Green nodded. "He has dyslexia. That *is* a problem."

"But he's real good at other stuff, like in math. They tested him, and Dad said he scored way high—like a genius."

Mrs. Green nodded again. "We'll have to get help from Special Education, Barney. I'll do what I can. It may be hard on him. The other children won't understand. But I'll do my best."

"Gee, thanks a lot! If you need anything, just send me a note, will you?"

She smiled and said very softly, "You look out for Joe, don't you, Barney?"

"I sure try to. Well, I'll be checking with you. And thanks a lot." I stuck my head back through the door for a second. "See you later, Joe," I called.

I hurried back to the main building feeling pretty good about Joe. That Mrs. Green was swell! Not like some of the old gripes we had back in our old school in Chicago. They probably had teachers like that here, too, though.

Joe and Jake stayed in the same room all day, because that was the way they did it in the elementary school. Since I was in junior high school, I went to different rooms for my classes. The first one was Room 111,

Mrs. Henderson, American history. When I went in, all the kids stared at me while I gave Mrs. Henderson the sheet from the office.

She was a heavy set black woman with gray hair. After reading the note, she stared hard at me through her gold-rimmed glasses. "You're getting a late start. Take a seat there." I sat down, and she told the class, "This is Barnabas Buck. He's from Chicago."

"A real city slicker!" somebody whispered, loud enough for the whole class to hear.

"Keep quiet, Junior Pote!" Mrs. Henderson said. "Here, take this book, Barney, and try to read all you can up to page 134. That's where we are."

Somehow I got through the class. After looking through the history book, I felt better. It wasn't the same book we'd used at the old school, but it was the same stuff in the book. Good thing they couldn't change history around too much.

The bell rang, and I made my way toward the door. Suddenly somebody crashed into my back, and I dropped my books. When I turned around, muddy little eyes were grinning at me. Junior Pote, the chunky kid who'd commented on my arrival. I knew that grin. I'd seen it on other faces before. It said, "Welcome to our little world, and get ready, 'cuz I'm gonna make life miserable for you."

So Arkansas isn't much different from Chicago, I

thought. Wherever you go, there's always a Junior Pote.

"Guess I'm just clumsy, Yankee boy," he said, a smirk on his round face. He waited for me to say something, but I just picked up my stuff and left. I heard him say something to the kid with him—a guy named Bubba Simmons—and they both laughed.

The rest of my classes were similar to what I'd had in Chicago, except that here algebra was taught in the ninth grade. Maybe I would be lucky enough to drop dead before I had to take it. I had general science with a young teacher named Mr. Franklin. My math teacher was named Dale Littlejohn, and he also taught in the P.E. Department. The kids called him Coach, and I liked him right off. He looked real cool—the way I wanted to look and never could.

Coach was fairly tall and had a good build, neat brown hair, a straight nose, and no freckles. He spent a little time with me in math class and wound up saying, "Well, you're not in too bad a shape, Barney. You may not set the curve, but there won't be any problems if you work hard." I was glad he called me Barney and was even gladder when I found out he'd be in charge of my P.E. class.

At noon Jake and I ate together. The third grade kids ate on a different schedule, so we didn't see Joe. I asked Jake how it was going and he shrugged. "Ah, what's the difference? Teachers are all the same."

Even though I was uptight about our being in Arkansas, I felt we were in a pretty good school. Everybody seemed real friendly, and the teachers and the principal seemed to be human beings.

When the bell rang for the first afternoon class, I said, "I'll see you at the bus. And Jake, don't get too buddy-buddy with anyone, OK?" He shrugged and went to his classroom.

My first afternoon class was English, a subject I had always done pretty well in. Unfortunately the teacher was a real wimpy guy named Burton. Unlike most of the other men teachers, he wore a suit instead of slacks and a jacket. Besides, he talked through his nose in a nasally whine.

After looking at me, he raised his eyebrows and said, "Well, I suppose I'll have to do the best I can with you." He hadn't seen even one of my papers and he'd already decided I was no good.

Some people you have to work at hating, but I hated X. J. Burton that first day. He was teaching sentence diagramming, which I was pretty good at. He kept calling on the same kids over and over, and they weren't even the smartest kids in class. Several kids kept raising their hands to go to the board, but he ignored them. He put one long sentence on the board and smirked at the class.

"Someday you'll be able to do this sort of sentence,"

he said. "Anyone want to attempt it now?" He looked around the room, then stared at me. "How about you, Barnabas? Why don't you show us how it's done in the big metropolis?"

I should have lain low, but several of the kids giggled and X. J. Burton joined them. I got up without a word and diagrammed the sentence on the board, letter perfect. Diagramming wasn't hard once you knew how, and I sort of enjoyed it. Then I sat down and looked at him.

"Well, we have a scholar in our midst." His words sounded like he was pleased, but the bright red color of his face let me know he was no such thing. I knew I'd made a bad mistake by doing a perfect job, but it was too late.

When the class was over, I tried to get away fast, but a girl was going through the door the same time I was. She whispered, "I'm glad you put Whistle Britches in his place!"

Her comment caught me off guard. She gave me a grin, and I noticed that though she wasn't a pretty girl, her skin was real nice and her teeth were nice and straight—which I admired because mine weren't. And she was tall. Almost as tall as I was.

"I'm Debra Simmons," she said when we were in the hall. "Maybe you can coach me on that stuff. I never have understood it."

I'd sometimes daydreamed about what I would do if a

girl ever showed any interest in me. I was so much taller than the girls my age that I thought I looked like a freak. I always wished I could be cool like Mel Gibson or Christian Slater. Well, now was my chance. Now a girl *was* showing some interest in me . . . and what did I do but mumble something about being pretty busy!

Wishing I could kick myself into next week, I excused myself and left at a lope to get away from her. I tried to tell myself it was because we couldn't afford to have any close friends that I'd treated her that way, but deep down I knew I was just a *jerk*.

I sat through study hall in a big room that was also the school library, then I went to P.E., my last class of the day. The gym was swarming with kids because two classes had to meet at the same time. I found Mr. Littlejohn and asked him what to do.

"Well, you need some equipment—shoes, shorts, the usual things. Did you play ball in Chicago?"

"Oh, just in gym class. I'm no good."

"Well, you're a tall one. Maybe you're a little clumsy now, but give yourself time." Then he called to the guys on the floor. He looked at me and said, "Look, Barney, just slip off your shoes. We're just fooling around today. You can join in and meet the rest of the guys."

I didn't want to, but I knew it was coming sooner or later. I took off my shoes and put them on the floor with my books and went to join the others.

"This is Barney Buck, you guys," Coach said, then had them introduce themselves one by one. "Look at that reach!" he added. "I say he's going to be a great center if he keeps growing. Let's see what we have."

Gym was OK. They tried me out, and sure enough I got bumped around some, but nothing bad. I wasn't really much good at basketball. At my old school, I'd held just about every position, but I was too slow. Besides, I couldn't dribble, and I wasn't a good passer. One thing I could do was make a jump shot. When they'd found that out back home, they'd let me just sort of play center. I would try to keep up going back and forth down the court—always behind the others—but if they got the ball to me and I was in position, I could usually go up, no matter what they did to me on defense, and put the ball in the basket.

The class was almost over, and I'd proven to the kids that I couldn't run, pass, or dribble. My team was losing, and, sort of by accident, one of the guys got desperate and threw me the ball. A good-looking kid named Tommy Randell was guarding me when I jumped up and put the ball in the basket. It just swooshed in without touching the rim.

Tommy had been making a monkey out of me the whole period. When I made the shot, he stopped and stared at me. "How'd you do that?" he demanded.

Coach started us again. A little kid on my team—

Ernie Jackson—waited until I got back in position after the other team scored, then fed me the ball. This time Tommy and another guy named Felix Simpkins tried to stop me. I put the ball in again, and then the whistle blew.

"Double foul, Tommy," Coach said. "What do you think you're doing? Next thing you'll try is using a hoe handle on defense!" Then he grinned at me and asked, "Can you make a free throw as good as a jump shot?"

"I'm just fair." But I took two, and they both sailed through—swishers—and a little murmur went around the guys.

That was the way it went. I couldn't run and I was clumsy, but I could make that jump shot. The other team kept fouling me, so I made points like crazy. Finally we quit, and the guys were all pretty nice, even those on the other side.

Tommy said, "Well, we may have to wheel you from one end of the court to the other in a wheelchair, but boy, can you pop that jump shot!"

Everyone else left for the showers, and I went over to get my shoes. "You're going to be a good one, Barney," Coach said. "When you get that lanky frame of yours coordinated, look out!"

I turned a little red and put one of my shoes on. Something was wrong with it; I pulled my foot out and looked down. Someone had filled it with black grease. I looked at the coach. He'd noticed it but didn't say a word. I guess he was waiting for me to cry about it or something, but I just grinned and said, "Guess somebody wanted to keep me from getting blisters."

He nodded slowly, a glint in his gray eyes. Then he grinned. "Come on down to the locker room, Barney. We have some old shoes there. You can make do until we get these cleaned up." We were almost down the stairs when he asked in an even tone, "Any idea who did it?"

Thinking back, I could recall two guys who had stopped to watch. They'd been near my shoes for a long time.

"I think I know."

When I didn't continue, he gave me a quick smile. "We've got a few here that would try something like that. Don't think it's the whole bunch."

He found a pair of sneakers that were pretty ripe—but they fit—and then got some paper to wrap my street shoes in. "See you, Barney. Come and see me if you need to."

On the whole, it's not bad, I thought on the way to the bus. *Not bad at all.* I knew I could handle the subjects, and there were enough good teachers to balance out the cruds.

I got to the bus stop, and my heart gave a lurch. Jake was sandwiched between the two I had already learned to dread: Junior Pote and Bubba Simmons. Each one had a paw on Jake's arm, and a crowd was gathered around. I hurried on over, and Bubba looked up with a mean grin. "Well, big brother, you came just in time. Your little brother here, he's been a *baaaaad* boy!"

"What's wrong, Jake?" I asked.

"Aw, nothing!" Jake said, trying to pull loose from the two without success. "They're just sore losers, that's all."

"Your brother hustled my little brother and most of the kids in his class out of their pocket money. We don't like that, Yankee boy!" Junior turned Jake loose, then came up to me and shoved his face close to mine. "You think you can come down and take us poor hillbillies with your big city ways?"

"It was all fair and square!" Jake said. He was angry and not scared like me. "I didn't cheat!"

"How'd he do it?" I asked Junior.

The girl I'd run away from earlier was standing close by, and she answered me. "Oh, he won their money with that silly tic-tac-toe," she said. She looked a lot like Bubba Simmons and they had the same last name, so I put two and two together and figured they were related.

At the mention of tic-tac-toe, I shook my head. Joe had figured out how to win every time, and Jake had talked him into showing him the trick. He'd cleaned up among the kids at school until they'd caught on. I don't know how Joe had done it, but he discovered that if you can go first *and* know how to start, there's no way the other kid can win. You put your *X* or your *O* in the middle square, and you can't lose. It's not cheating exactly, but it's not far from it when you know what's going on and the other kid doesn't.

We had to get out of this thing fast, so I said, "Jake, you know what Dad told you he'd do to you if you ever did that stupid thing again?" He stared at me for a second, then got that sullen look of his. I went on as hard as I could. "You give that money back right now, and maybe I won't fink on you."

He scowled but started giving the change back to the kids who had crowded around. "Sorry about that," I said to them. "He's just a kid and has to be watched."

Bubba and Junior didn't like it. They glanced at each other and were about to do something when the bus driver came around the bus and said, "Come on! We haven't got all day."

I got on the bus, pulling Jake after me. Joe was already on, and I took a deep breath when the bus pulled out. Bubba and Junior were glaring at me, but Debra gave me a grin and a little wave, which I didn't dare respond to, especially with her brother standing there.

We got home just before dark. By the time we had fixed supper and done homework and taken baths in the old claw-footed bathtub, I was beat. I thought for a long time about the million things that had to be done, and it seemed pretty grim!

"I had a *good* time at school today, Barney," Joe said at bedtime. "Mrs. Green really likes me, I think. She seemed real surprised when I showed her how to find square roots."

"Well, that's good, Joe."

"We can stay here together now, can't we?"

"Well, if everything goes right, Joe."

He was quiet for a few minutes. "Do you think it will be all right if I pray about it?"

I gave his head a rub. "I believe that will be all right, Joe."

I wished I could pray about everything, too, but I figured I didn't really deserve to talk to God considering all the stuff I'd been doing that he wouldn't like. So I just gave Joe a tired smile and said, "While you're at it, put in a word for me, will you?"

I needed it.

5
The Mortgage

WHEN we first got to Goober Holler, we lived like the guy in the circus who does the balancing act with the plates spinning on tall sticks. He gets one of the plates started with a flip of his wrist. Then another and another. Just about the time he's got most of them spinning around, the *first* plate has just about run out of speed and is ready to fall off. So what does he do? He runs back and gives it a new spin. But there's another one ready to fall! Then he runs from one to the other like a crazy man trying to keep all the plates spinning at the same time, and he looks headed for a *mess!*

Well, that's about how it was with us. We had to keep the judge in Chicago happy; we had to keep Miss Jean convinced that we were doing great; we had to keep Cedarville thinking that the Bucks were a complete family with parents and all. On top of that we had to keep house, do the cooking, wash our clothes, pay the bills, and about ten million other things.

The money problem alone almost drove me up the wall! Miss Jean had given me three hundred dollars when we'd left Chicago. That would do us, she'd said, until arrangements could be made to set up an account. But that money was nearly gone the first week. The gas alone cost about that much.

What I did still gives me cold chills. Miss Jean had gone over the figures with me. After our old house was sold, the money would be put into a trust fund for our college. Dad had taken out an insurance policy on himself, and after the bills were paid there was about thirty-five thousand dollars for us. That sounded like a fortune to me, but Miss Jean said it would be invested and the interest on it would be about three hundred dollars a month. Then she told me that whoever kept us would get one hundred dollars a month for each of us, plus whatever the state paid.

That would suit us just fine when the money came in. But it didn't do us much good when we were completely broke after the first week. I knew I had to do something, and what I did wasn't illegal exactly, but it wasn't right. I made Jake write a letter to Miss Jean in the same handwriting he'd used before, and then sign it *Roy Buck.* I told him to say things were a little tight and if she could give us an extra amount, it would make things a lot easier. Jake threw in some stuff on his own about how much it cost to get started in school and so on.

In about a week a three hundred dollar check made out to Roy Buck arrived. I put it in the bank, but I couldn't sleep for two or three days. Miss Jean said that the state would also be sending more money, but that was different. I figured the insurance money was Roy Buck's own money, and Dad would have wanted us to have it.

The money helped us buy some used furniture. We found a heating stove for twenty dollars at a junk furniture store. A moving sale just about saved us, thanks to a family that practically gave their stuff away. We got a table and four chairs, a couch and easy chair, two complete beds with mattresses and springs, dishes that didn't match too well, rusty old yard and garden tools, and lots of other stuff. We got it all for fifty-five dollars, and Jake conned the man into hauling it to our place for nothing.

The first three weeks we worked like slaves. I learned how to put glass in the rest of the broken windows. We gave the old place a real cleaning and spent a lot of time clearing the bushes and weeds that had grown up in the yard. Of course we had to do the work after school and on weekends.

Jake balked once, but I just stuck my face in his. "Are you ready to go back to Chicago?" I asked. "I bet Judge Poindexter can find you a real nice home where you won't have to work!"

That shut him up.

The good one was Joe. He never complained once, and I never heard a word about television. He would ask me to read stories to him, which I always did anyway, and he just about kept up with me and Jake on the work. Joe had always liked to fiddle around with tools and stuff, and he did a lot of things that helped.

He'd watched Dad fix things, and Joe learned fast. He fixed our faucet in the kitchen sink when Jake couldn't do a thing with it. When the stove we bought wouldn't burn, Joe took it apart and found out that it had the wrong-sized hole in one of the parts. He figured out how to change it, and that stove worked fine!

Joe was looking better, too. He had a good color and was smiling a lot.

During those first weeks nobody came to see us. Most people didn't know we lived there, I guess. The road was almost invisible it was so overgrown, and there really weren't any close neighbors. That suited us just fine.

The first Sunday I roused Jake and Joe, and we all

went to church. It was a little, white frame church about two miles from Cedarville, which meant that we had a long walk. There weren't many people there, but the man who taught our class, Mr. Terry, was nice. Of course we had to tell them that our parents were gone a lot; "Mom" wasn't well and was staying with relatives in Illinois, and "Dad" had a traveling job and was gone most of the time.

Telling and living a lie like we'd been doing was bad enough, but doing it in church was worse! I let Jake do it, since he lied better than I did and it didn't bother him as much.

Anyway, before long the preacher brought his wife to visit us. All it took, though, was one time wading down that overgrown muddy road and they were discouraged—especially when they found out that nobody was there but us kids. I figured they wouldn't be back very often!

A family named Stover lived about three miles north on the highway. They came by and brought their kids, just to be neighborly, but they didn't stay long. As they were leaving, Jake gave them something to think about.

"I hope they stay in the middle of the road and don't step on any of the mines," he whispered to me, making sure he said it loud enough for them to hear.

"Mines?" Mr. Stover said, looking up.

"Oh, it ain't nothin'. I don't reckon they'd go off," Jake explained.

"Go off!" Mrs. Stover screamed. "You mean there are explosives in the road?"

"Well, Pa was a little nervous about leaving us alone so much, so he got these things from the army surplus store in Little Rock. I think they're so old they probably wouldn't go off anyway, and we usually take 'em up when Pa comes back, but we can't always remember where they are. Just keep to the middle of the road." Jake gave me a puzzled look. "Barney, we did put those things at the *edge* of the road, didn't we?"

"All except for two, I think." I tried to look serious. "Anyway there's a good chance that all this rain has ruined them. But I'd be careful, Mrs. Stover. Never can tell."

They looked at each other and then at us. Without a word, they went on their way and didn't use the road at all. They waded alongside of it, getting slapped in the face with bushes and buried up to the knees in red gumbo mud. I could hear Mr. Stover saying something like "You kids stay away from these crazy people! You hear me?"

We later found out that the Stovers had not only told about the mines, but had also added a lot of other stuff about how dangerous we were. That was what we wanted, but it was going to be pretty lonesome.

About three or four days after that, we got another visitor: our friend Clyde Rodgers. He came in with an empty truck on his way to Fort Worth to catch a big auction. He had to hear all about what we'd been doing, and he nearly split his sides over the Stover incident. We talked until late; then when Jake and Joe had gone to bed, he waited until they got quiet before he said, "Barney, I've been to see Miss Jean two or three times."

"What about?" I asked quickly. Maybe some people learn to put their conscience to sleep as time passes, but mine was worse than ever. Every time I thought about Miss Jean, I thought about how we'd had to tell her things that weren't so. It was like a red-hot iron touching me whenever Clyde mentioned her name.

"Oh, just to tell her about what's going on down here. You know, sort of string her along."

He saw I didn't like it, so he added quickly, "Oh, I didn't actually tell her much, Barney."

I was angry with Clyde, and that was silly since *I* was the one responsible for the whole thing. I couldn't even blame it on Jake, which I'd already tried. "You *had* to tell her something, Clyde." Then I shook my head and went on as if to myself, "Whatever you said wasn't the truth."

"Ahhh, come *on,* Barney!" Clyde said. He leaned across the table where we were sitting, his face serious looking for once. "Look, I know all this is botherin' you. I mean about what you had to do to keep the family together. And I can see that. I mean, nobody *likes* to lie!

But sometimes, Barney, there's no other way! I mean, you gotta do whatever is necessary . . ."

Clyde was pretty upset. I thought about how he'd taken our part, helping us when he hadn't really had to. "Sure, I know," I said. "Clyde, it'll be all right, I guess."

We finally went to bed, and I tried to sleep. Just when I was about to doze off, the most awful noise I ever heard broke out right in our front yard. It sounded like a hundred dogs fighting. When I jumped up and looked out the window, I could see that a whole pack of dogs was gathered around the big oak tree in our front yard.

"What in the world?" I asked. Jake and Joe ran to the window. We didn't know what was going on.

"Look, somebody's coming!" Joe said.

I ran over and grabbed the twelve-gauge shotgun, and Jake snatched up the Browning .22 rifle Clyde had bought from Johnson's Hardware. Someone was hollering now. I went downstairs and turned the porch light on. There were at least two people I knew—Junior Pote and Bubba Simmons—as well as a couple of other boys about my age and about five or six men. I was pretty scared, but I knew we had to do something. I opened the front door and stood on the porch.

"What do you think you're doing?" I hollered as loud as I could. Some of them must've heard me over the din, or maybe they'd seen the light, because one of the men looked my way and came over.

"Well, by gum, I'd clean forgot that this place was being lived in!" He was a large man with a big nose and good-sized teeth. His face was fat with small eyes that reminded me of pigs' eyes. He came up close to the porch. "Why, I guess you're the Buck young'uns, ain't you?"

"That's right," I said. "What are you doing here in the middle of the night disturbing us?"

"Why, boy, we're coon huntin'! Matter of fact, my boy told me you was here, and I meant to send word over for you boys and your pa to come and join in with us tonight. Plumb slipped my mind." He shoved a big hand at me, and I shook it. "My name's Emmett Simmons." He waved his hand around. "I own most of the land around here. All except this place, matter of fact." He glanced toward the house. "Where's your pa?"

"He's asleep. Been on a trip and is just worn out."

"That so? Well, it's only about nine. He sure ain't sleeping with all these dogs making a racket! It'll be to his advantage to let me have a word with him tonight. Look, we're gonna build a fire right down the road, over by the creek bridge." He pointed toward the west. "Tell your pa to come over, and he can meet up with some of the men, and you boys can get a taste of coon huntin'."

"I'll tell him," I said.

"Good!" He went back to the dogs, and I heard him say, "There ain't no coon there, boys. That there's a slick tree. That ol' smoky dog has lied to me again. Let's git over to the branch and build us a fire."

Then they all left, cutting straight through the woods. Jake and Joe crowded in close. "You gonna go, Barney?" Jake asked.

"Maybe I'd better," I said.

Just then Clyde came out, rubbing his eyes. "What in the world was that racket?"

"Bunch of coon hunters," I answered. "One of them wants to talk to our dad. You feel like going out and seeing what he wants?"

"Might as well," Clyde grumbled. "Can't get to sleep after a racket like that!"

He and I got dressed and then went down the road. We stopped when we saw their fire by the edge of the woods. Mr. Simmons spotted us right away. He had eyes like a hawk. "Buck! Come on over here! You fellers move and make room for this man."

He had us sit down by the fire, all the time pointing out the hunters: "That's Marvin Hembree. That there's Alex Templeton. That's his brother Tom. Mace Perry, Acie Little, and this is my boy, Bubba. That's Junior Pote, Roger Hembree, and Les Springer. This here is Mr. Roy Buck and his boy Barney."

Everyone was staring at us, and we had to make it look good. We nodded in a general way, said, "Pleased to meet you," and waited for Mr. Simmons to go on.

He sat down, and everyone began to talk about the dogs. I couldn't understand it—not a word about business. The dogs were out in the woods, far off. Those men couldn't even see them, but they knew them by their voices.

Mace Perry listened and said, "That's Jenny. I reckon she's got a varmint this time."

After a while Les spat in the fire and cursed. "I knowed that dog was goin' to be no good. Jes' listen to him carry on over that cold trail."

For a long time I sat there listening to the dogs while their owners told stories about what dogs had done in other hunts and about what had happened at a certain place or on a particular trail.

It was strange. I had never even *seen* a coon, much less a coon dog, that I could remember. I'd never been out of Chicago or in the woods around a campfire.

Right there, sitting in the dark and drinking bitter coffee out of a tin cup, I knew for sure I was going to learn to hunt coons in the woods with a dog. Somehow I knew that I could do it! I knew I would be good at it and that, good or not, it was something I had to try.

Of course, I didn't say a word then, or even later, to anybody else. If *I* thought I was crazy, no telling what other people would think.

Then Mr. Simmons said, "Come here, Gyp." A dog that I hadn't seen came out of the dark and stood between Mr. Simmons and me. "You know dogs, Buck?" he asked Clyde.

I looked at the dog and reached out to touch his smooth side. He was a dark black-and-tan. When I touched his head, he turned to look at me. I could see his eyes by the light of the fire. He was the prettiest thing I'd ever seen. I made another vow. I was going to have a dog.

"No, he don't know dogs," Clyde said after glancing at me. "Grew up in the city. Couldn't have dogs there."

"That's too bad," Mr. Simmons said. "Dogs are nice to have. I got a few myself."

"I reckon that's the understatement of the year!" one of the men said as the others gave a low laugh.

Mr. Simmons was a big dog man—raised them and sold them. He began telling about one dog after another, and though I didn't understand a lot of it, I knew this was a world that I *had* to enter!

Finally Mr. Simmons got up, stretched, and said, "Buck, let's you and me take a little walk. These lies is gettin' too deep to swim in!"

He walked off, and Clyde gave me a nod. He and I followed Mr. Simmons, who stopped at a big tree near a wire fence.

"I want to buy your place, Buck," he said to Clyde. I glanced at Clyde and could tell he was taken off guard.

"I could beat around the bush and try to get the price down, but I don't do things that way."

Clyde caught my glance. I shook my head, and he understood right away. "Mr. Simmons, I gotta tell you. The place ain't for sale."

Simmons waved a muscular hand in the air and gave a tolerant smile. "Sure, sure, I know. That's the way we play the game. You want more, I'll give less. But let me tell you a few things about your place. First, it's landlocked."

"Landlocked?"

"That means you can't get to it from the highway without crossing somebody's land. In this case, you have to cross my land. That road that leads to your place? That's through my land. I put the road in myself. You have an easement, but it's still landlocked. And again, the land isn't good for anything but timber. You can't farm it, can't make pastureland."

"Well, I could raise timber," Clyde said.

"You don't have enough land for that, Buck. Takes a thousand acres for a man to make it. Now I'll lay my cards on the table. I want your land. When I get it, I'll own the whole section. I'll pay you the top dollar, even *more.*" He spread his hands out. "I ain't *never* been an easy man in a deal, but this time I know what I want and I got the money to pay for it—and a bonus of five thousand dollars on top. Now you can't beat that!"

It was a good deal. I suspected it was more than a fair offer and that Emmett Simmons didn't go around making deals like that every day. But I knew there was no way we could take it. We were living on the thin edge of trouble anyway. If we tried to sell land—legal business—Judge Poindexter would smell it out in a minute flat!

Clyde gave me a look, and I shook my head just a little. "Well, thanks for your offer, Mr. Simmons," said Clyde. "I know it's a good one, but I don't aim to sell. And I would appreciate it if you don't bring it up again."

I'd never seen a man change so fast. One second Mr. Simmons was nice and easygoing. Then his eyes got even smaller, and his mouth looked like a knife edge. He leaned toward Clyde as if he were going to hit him.

"All right, Buck!" His voice was harsh and mean. "I tried to be nice about it. Now I'll show you I can be the other way. I don't suppose you know anything about the note I hold on your place?"

"No, I don't know anything about it," Clyde said.

Neither did I.

"I didn't figure you did," he sneered. "Well, just to inform you, James Buck borrowed five thousand dollars from me at 10 percent three years ago. It was to be paid off one thousand dollars a year plus interest on the first day of the year. He made one payment, then died. I guess last year's payment was made out of this estate from the rent the place brought in. But if you don't make that payment on time, your place is *mine!* I've been asking around, and it looks like you got a mighty slim chance of makin' a living there, much less making a big payment!"

Mr. Simmons didn't know just *how* slim!

Clyde glanced at me and shrugged. "I'll take care of it."

"See you do!" he snapped and turned to join the other hunters.

Clyde and I went back to the house, and Jake and Joe met us at the door. When I told them about the note, it was like throwing cold water on their faces. We just sort of fell apart.

"A thousand dollars!" Joe breathed. "Where are we going to get it?"

"Be more than that with the interest," I replied.

"Maybe we can borrow it from the bank," Jake said.

"How would we pay *that* back?" I snapped.

We sat there in the silence of our own worry. I felt I ought to offer some hope, since I was the oldest, but I couldn't think of anything. We could hear the coon dogs howling and the trees scratching at the windows.

"Let's go to bed," I said after a while. "We'll think of something." Some inspiring speech! I was too low myself to cheer them up.

Clyde gave me a pat on the shoulder, but he didn't have any answers, either.

"Don't worry, Barney," Joe said after we were in bed. "I'll tell God about it. He's got plenty of money."

"I wonder what interest *he* charges?" Jake mumbled, half-asleep.

6
The Black-and-Tan Hound

I got it!" Jake shouted as he scrambled off the bus one day after school, his face lit up like a neon sign.

"You always do," I said grumpily as we walked down the road toward our house. We were into our fifth week of school, and I was feeling pretty down. We'd all done OK with our grades. In fact, Miss Jean had sent us a letter saying how pleased the judge had been with our progress. And our house was looking like a real home, inside and out. But I was still feeling sort of bad.

"What's wrong with you?" Jake asked. "You worried about that ol' mortgage?"

"It doesn't make me too happy thinking about it," I replied. As a matter of fact, that wasn't it. That problem was nine months off, and our biggest problems were right *now.* "Have you heard any of those rumors people are telling about us?"

Jake gave me one of his goofy grins and said, "Sure! They're *great,* ain't they? I hope they get worse!"

"Worse!" I stared at him. "Did you hear we're shooting at anyone who gets near our place? How can it get worse than *that?"*

"Well, it'll keep people from dropping in, won't it?"

"It won't keep the sheriff from dropping by!" Joe piped up.

"I hope he does. It'll make us even more dangerous if the law has to watch us!"

"Yeah, I guess so." I knew it made sense to make hermits out of ourselves. The less we saw of people, the more chance the Master Plan had. But it was pretty lonesome. I'd never been run over with friends, but now I had to build a wall around myself so that even when a chance came to make friends, I couldn't take it. And as far as I could see, we would have to fake our way until we were grown!

"Did you hear the one about us stealing dogs?" Jake asked.

"What!"

"Sure, that's what people are saying."

"Well, I heard people talking about animals disappearing all over the country, but I thought that had been going on a long time—before we even came here."

"Well, the way it goes is this: Old Roy Buck has been comin' here for a long time to steal in secret. Now he's got such a good thing going that he's brought his whole bunch of boys here to help him steal more."

I couldn't believe it. "Nobody would swallow that story! Why would we do that?"

"'Them Bucks is all no good and crazy,'" Jake said out of the side of his mouth. He made believe he was spitting tobacco juice, just like old man Jenkins, the town gossip. "'Them fellers is *bad!* You ever see that Roy Buck come out and look right at you? No, siree! He sneaks around like he was afraid he was gonna get caught at it. That's what. I'll tell you when he does business—after dark. That's when!'"

"Is that what they're saying?" I sounded surprised, but I knew Jake was right. People had been giving me funny looks whenever I'd gone into town and done business. I had acted funny, and the suspicion was fired by the gossip.

"Don't worry, Barney, we'll make out without anybody. And don't worry. We'll make that thousand-dollar payment."

"Let me guess . . . you have a plan."

"It can't miss! I'll tell you about it when we get home."

When we'd gotten off the bus, only a few of the kids had said, "See you tomorrow." They wouldn't meet my eyes, and I knew they'd been hearing the stories about us. Jake hadn't noticed, but Joe was not happy about it. The little Carlton boy he'd been sitting near most every day had deliberately ignored him today and gone to sit with Dave Morris.

Halfway to the house, we came across a big tree lying right across the road. "Hey, look at *that!*" Jake said. It was a big pine tree around three feet in diameter. It hadn't been there when we'd left for school in the morning. We took a quick look around and found several stumps and the tops of trees.

"Loggers have been here. These are the skidder tracks," I said.

"Sure, but why didn't they take this one?" Joe asked. "We can't get by."

"I think I know why," I said slowly. "Mr. Simmons owns this land. He's making it tough on us so we'll sell the place."

"Well, that old crook!" Jake shouted. Then he kicked the big tree and hurt his foot. He began to hop around, calling Emmett Simmons a few other names.

"Well, you ought to go thank him, Jake!" I said. "You were interested in keeping people away, and not too many are going to get by this tree."

We didn't have any trouble because we could duck under it, but no vehicle was going to get by as long as the tree was there. "He'll have to move it," I said. "I think it's the law. He just wants to make things as hard as he can."

We finally got to the house and started to do the chores. "What's your great scheme this time, Jake?" I asked. "The one that's going to pay the note off?"

"Oh, yeah!" Jake said, his face getting bright. "Well, I've been talking to a kid named Alfred Dennison. Last year his dad let him have a little patch of ground, and he planted watermelons in it. He sold them for about two dollars apiece and really made a pile!"

"We don't know anything about raising melons," Joe said.

"There's nothing to it," Jake said. "You know that big field right behind the house? Why, it's perfect. You just pop the seeds in the ground and let the melons grow, then pull 'em and sell 'em. We can't miss!"

"I've heard that before," I said.

"It'll work!" Jake insisted. "Look, I found out all about it from the kid. You get the seeds for almost nothing. You have to have a big field—just like ours. You don't have to plow or anything, I tell you. And there's a good market for melons. No trouble at all to sell. There's only one thing I can't figure out."

"Aha!" I said. "What's the hitch?"

"Well, according to Alfred, when the melons get ripe, some animals will mess them up, like armadillos and even coons."

"You have to stay up and watch them at night?" Joe asked.

"Nah, we couldn't do that." Jake shook his head. "I asked Alfred what we could do, and he said the best way was to get a good dog."

Suddenly I perked up. It was just another scheme until then, but I hadn't forgotten for a day my desire to get a dog. I hadn't wanted to mention it, because I knew it would cost a lot and I didn't want to be selfish. But now I had a good *reason.* And if we needed a dog, why, we'd just pick up one that could hunt coons, too!

"I think it's a great idea!" I said. "The best you ever had! As a matter of fact, we need a dog for lots of things. I still think somebody is sneaking around the house sometimes, and a dog would keep him away, whoever he is."

"I know he's out there, Barney," Joe said suddenly. "I've seen him."

Jake and I stared at each other. "Uh, Joe. . . ," I said.

"No, really," he said, a serious look on his face. "I saw him twice. Both times it was real early in the morning. He was going through the woods and stayed back pretty far, but I saw him. I couldn't see his face, but he was tall and skinny. I bet he's the one who slept in the bed here. He's probably some kind of criminal."

I didn't think Joe had seen anybody, but it gave me another reason for buying a dog. "Well, that settles it. I'll get us a dog!"

The next day after school I asked around a little about dogs, and what I came up with was Emmett Simmons. Much as I hated the thought of going there, I found myself getting off the bus at his big farm, just a couple of miles north of Cedarville. A big paved driveway led up to a big house with white pillars out front, and the yard looked like a park.

I felt like a tramp when I went up the porch steps and rang the bell. Bubba opened the door and said, "What do *you* want?" Then I really felt like running.

"I need to see your father," I said, trying to keep my cool.

"What about?"

"Maybe I'd better tell him."

He stared at me, and I think he would have sent me away, but a woman came to the door. "What is it?" she said.

"I'd like to see Mr. Simmons, ma'am," I said in my most polite tone.

"He's out back with the dogs." She was red-faced and tall, with a nice smile. Bubba looked like his dad, and Debra looked like her mother, which was lucky for Debra!

“Thank you, ma’am,” I said and walked around the house. Out back were a bunch of little houses—dog houses—and almost every one of them had a dog on a chain lying close to it. Mr. Simmons was bending over. Mustering up my courage, I went over to him. “Hello, Mr. Simmons.”

He straightened up and looked at me carefully. “Your pa send you?”

“No, sir.”

“Well, what you want?” he snapped. I knew he’d been hoping that Roy Buck had decided to sell.

I heard someone come up behind me, so I turned around. It was Bubba. “Well, I . . . I’d sort of like to see a dog,” I said barely above a whisper.

“Speak up, boy. See a dog?” Mr. Simmons said. “Well, look around you, boy.”

“No, sir, I mean—well, I haven’t got much money, but I’d like to *buy* a dog, if they don’t cost too much.”

Bubba gave a hateful laugh. “How about that, Pa? *He* wants to buy a dog.” He stared at me. “You know what a good dog costs, Yankee boy?”

“No.”

“Some come as high as five thousand dollars,” he said.

My heart sank. “Oh,” I said and started to leave. “Well, I didn’t know they cost that much.”

“Wait just a minute,” Mr. Simmons said, with a gleam

in his eye. "Lots of dogs cost that much, but not all. What sort of dog do you want?"

"I dunno. Maybe like that one." I pointed to the dog he was holding.

He laughed. "Well, I reckon you *would!* So would every other coon hunter in the country. This here is Midnight, best dog I got. He'll win every prize in the country if I know my dogs." Then he glanced at me. "You want a huntin' dog?"

"Well, just a good dog, like one who would be a watch-dog. I sure would like to have a real hunting dog. I don't have a lot of money, though. Only about fifty dollars."

"Well, now, ordinarily that wouldn't buy you much of a dog," he said and began rubbing his chin. "But I just had a thought." He looked at Bubba. "What about that young dog we got left from this litter?"

Bubba looked at him, then at me. "Well, he's still here, but he's worth more than fifty dollars."

"Sure he is, but we got too many dogs now," his father said.

Bubba glared at me. "He don't know nothing 'bout dogs. That dog is outta the same litter as Midnight. He ought to be sold to a *real* hunter!"

"Oh, come on now, Son. Everybody's gotta start somewhere. Barney here ain't had no chance, being raised in town and all. I say we act big about it and give him his chance."

"It's your say, Daddy," Bubba said. "I wouldn't do it."

"Come on, boy," Mr. Simmons said to me. "I'll show you the dog." As we walked toward the far side of the houses, he told me about the dogs. "Them is Walkers there. And that one, he's a redbone. Both good coon dogs. See those pups? They're bluetick hounds."

We came to some houses that were a little run-down. "We house the older dogs here," Mr. Simmons said. We stopped by one of the houses, and a dog got up to meet us. He acted as if nobody had paid him any attention for a long time, and he strained at the chain.

"That's a black-and-tan," Mr. Simmons said. "Finest coon dog in the world for my money."

The dog's fur was black with a bluish tinge, except for his muzzle and feet. These were a soft brown, like a fine suede jacket. He had a glossy coat and clear, bright eyes. His tail was held above his back, and he looked wide-awake, not cowed like some dogs. He must have weighed about fifty pounds, because he was really muscled for a young dog. I'd never seen anything more beautiful.

"He's registered, too. Same sire and dam as Midnight. Can't get no better bred dog nowhere," Mr. Simmons said.

I put my hand out, and the dog sniffed at it. Then he licked it and tried to get closer to me. He was probably lonesome and would have done that to anybody, but suddenly I had to have him!

"Well, like I told you, Mr. Simmons. . . ," I said.

"Sure, boy, I know. Well, let's see." He paused, and the dog kept straining to get close to me. I held my breath. Then he finally said, "Well, I must be gettin' senile, but you can have the dog for fifty dollars. You'll never get a bargain like that in a million years. You got the money?"

"Yes, sir!" I pulled the bills out of my pocket and gave them to him.

"You might as well take him now, I reckon. Come on, and I'll get his papers for you."

I couldn't believe it! As he untied the dog and handed me the rope, I felt almost dizzy. *My own coon dog!* I tried not to grin or cry, but I wanted to do both as we went to a little brick building.

The dog was sticking close to my legs. Then I noticed he was limping. "What's wrong with his leg?" I asked.

"What?" Mr. Simmons replied. "Oh, you mean that limp. I think he maybe got a thorn in a foot. They do that, you know. Should work itself out in a day or two," he added matter-of-factly.

He led me inside. A desk, a filing cabinet, and shelves filled with all sorts of medicines and shampoos for dogs stood against one wall. Nearby was a special tub for dogs. Another wall was almost covered with ribbons.

Mr. Simmons got some papers out of the filing cabinet and began filling them out.

"Did you win these at dog shows, Mr. Simmons?" I asked.

He looked up and grinned. "Not dog shows, boy. Field trials for hunting dogs. See, there's all kinds of contests. We take the dogs out and there's judges and the best dog wins the prize. There's local hunts and regionals and the National. Last year the National was at Pine Bluff, not fifty miles from here. I almost won it, too! I'll win it this year with Midnight! Grand prize is five thousand dollars!"

He handed me the papers and showed me where to sign them. "You have to mail this in to this address, and in about a month you'll get the papers back. Cost you $7.50 to get the official registration."

"Thanks a *lot,* Mr. Simmons." He just nodded, and I hurried out to get my dog.

He's got to have a good name, I thought as I untied him. We left, and he kept nibbling at me all the way to the entrance of the Simmonses' property. He almost knocked me down as he pushed in close to me.

By now he was limping pretty bad. "I'll get that thorn out when we get home, boy," I said. When we got to the highway, I realized I would probably have to walk the rest of the way. I got a ride pretty often, but now the way people were talking about us Bucks, it didn't seem likely that I would catch a ride from anyone around here.

Near the big gates, I met Debra Simmons. She looked very surprised at seeing me.

"Hello," I said. I had similar brilliant remarks handy so I could just let them drop when I wanted to impress somebody.

"Why, hello, Barney," she said, giving me a grin. "Stand right there, will you?" I didn't know what she meant, until she came and stood in front of me. She looked up at me and finally sighed. "My that feels *good!*"

"What feels good?"

"Looking up at a boy. I'm so much taller than the boys in my class that I feel like a *mother* to them! Sure is good to be around a really tall guy!"

"Well . . ." I tried to think of a clever remark, but none came. I finally said, "It would be better if I were *shorter,* instead of being a bean pole."

That's right. Put yourself down, I thought.

She laughed. "You'll grow out of *that.* I mean, you'll get heavier as you get older." Then she gave me a big sigh and looked worried. "But I'm never going to get any shorter."

"Shorter? Why would you want to be shorter? You look just right to me."

She got a little red, and then I did, too. She didn't say, "Do you *really* think so?" the way a lot of girls would. She just looked up and gave me a little smile. Then she looked behind me. "Oh, you've got the cripple."

I looked down at the dog, then back at her. "The cripple?"

"He's such a nice dog." She stooped down to stroke his head. "Too bad about his leg."

I felt like I was drowning and nobody was there to throw me a rope. "What's wrong with his leg?"

She rubbed his head and then stood up again, her brown eyes soft with pity. "Oh, he's got a bad leg. Guess you saw him limp."

"How'd he get it?"

"He was born with it, Barney. Dad usually has dogs put away when they're faulted like that, but he said . . ." Her voice trailed off, and her hand flew to her mouth. She glanced at the dog, then at me. "Oh, Barney!"

I pulled away from her, black anger building up inside me. "I guess he said, 'We'll get something for him from some dumb sucker who don't know beans.' Isn't that about it?" I knew Debra had had nothing to do with it, but when you get hurt, I guess you just hit whatever's near. "Think you're pretty smart, don't you? All you Simmonses are just too smart to live!"

"Debra, you come on in!" Bubba said with a mean grin on his fat red face. I whirled around.

"Well, who died and made you king?" Debra snapped. She turned and was going to say something to me, but Bubba grabbed her and pulled her toward the house. "Yankee boy has to git home, sister. He's gonna be a real coon hunter with that three-legged dog!" He laughed so hard he nearly bent over, and I had to get away.

I almost ran down the road, and Bubba kept laughing and laughing. I thought I heard Debra saying something to me, but I just kept on running.

When I was finally out of sight, I slowed down, out of breath. The dog was still limping alongside me. I walked with my head down, my face burning. *What a dumb thing to do!* I thought. *If they ever give awards for stupidity, wouldn't I be a winner!*

Then the dog whimpered and pressed against me. I stopped to look down at him. He was looking up at me, one paw touching my leg. Then he howled as if he thought he'd done something wrong and didn't know what it was.

I knelt down and put my arms around him. We stayed there for a while.

I thought about a name for him and finally decided to call him Tim. We'd been reading a book called *A Christmas Carol* in English class, and he reminded me of Tiny Tim, the kid with a crippled leg.

"It's not your fault, boy," I finally said. "You can't help it if you've got a bad leg, and I can't help being stupid." Then I got up, and we started on the long trip home. "Well, boy, you've sure found the right home. We're all losers out at Goober Holler. Join the club!"

7
A Special Visit

OUR first spring in Goober Holler surprised us.

"Look! It's snowing!" Joe called out one day. We all stopped and looked at the white in the trees, but I knew what it was. The dogwood trees had popped out with white blossoms, and against the black limbs of the oaks and hickories, it did look like snow. And it had all happened almost overnight.

One day the weather had been cold, damp, and miserable. The next day the ground felt warm to your feet, the sun was hot on your face, and the woods were touched with every color you could think of. The plum trees had turned pink, the wild violets were spots of lavender sprouting up all over the place, and the tiny yellow daffodils looked like Christmas decorations on the winter grass.

I was out every night with Tim. He didn't know any more than I did about hunting, but we both went wild when we went through the woods. Tim wasn't crippled too badly. His left hind leg was just stiff when he ran, and it made him wiggle from side to side. He was pretty fast, but not as fast as a dog with four good legs.

Running through the woods with Tim put me in good shape. Working a lot on the place did, too. One time in gym, Coach grabbed my arm and said, "Barney, you're putting some meat on that long frame."

Coach always had a good word for me, and one thing we did was start going to his church in town. He taught the class I was in and was about the best teacher I'd ever had! He could tell about old David and Goliath in a way that made me sit on the edge of my seat. He always came out to our place on Sundays, brought us to church, then took us back. He was one of the best friends we had.

As for Joe, he was doing fine. His teacher was always letting him make things and explain them to the class. He would make something in a workroom at the back of our house. But better than anything was that he had started sleeping with no bad dreams at all!

Jake was trying out different things. He started raising rabbits—to make millionaires of us—but the mama rabbit lost her mind and ate the babies. After that he organized a group of smaller boys to go all over town begging scrap metal. Once they got a bunch, they took it to the scrap yard and sold it. That seemed promising, until the boys figured out they didn't need a manager to take half the profit for none of the work, so that was *that*.

I begged Jake not to do something that would attract attention to us, and he said he wouldn't. I knew how much *that* promise was worth!

The day we planted the watermelon seeds was a nice day in mid-April. Jake had found out that if you planted on Easter, you could expect to be eating watermelon by the Fourth of July. We waited until it was late in the afternoon before going out to the empty field.

We had a good time putting the seeds in, then ended up shouting and throwing clods at each other. I was just pulling back a nice big clod when I heard a truck coming down the road. I'd asked Jake to write Mr. Simmons a letter about getting his logging crew to move the tree off of the road, but nothing came of it. We'd just continued to crawl under the tree, and I guessed nobody else cared. I thought maybe someone was coming to take the tree away.

It turned out to be a Jeep instead of a truck. I almost jumped when I saw Debra Simmons sitting next to an old man with a full white beard.

They pulled up close to the field and got out. A blue-tick hound followed them. The dog and Tim circled each other the way dogs do when they first meet.

"Hello, Barney," Debra said, seeming a little embarrassed. I'd stayed away from her at school pretty much, so I guessed she was thinking about the way I'd talked to her last time.

"Hello, Debra," I said. "What are you doing way out here?"

"Oh, nothing." I knew that wasn't true. "This is my granddad. Granddad, this is Barney Buck. And that's Jake, and that's Joe."

He stuck out his right hand, which felt hard as a file. *He sure doesn't look like his son,* I thought. He was tall—about six feet two—and lean as a pine tree. His skin was burned red, and he had about a million weather wrinkles on his face. His cheekbones were high, and peering out from under bushy silver brows were the sharpest, darkest eyes I'd ever seen.

"Hello, Barney," he said. I felt he was making up his mind about us. Finally he gave a little nod, then looked at the field. "Good field for watermelons. I remember your grandfather had a good patch here once. Must have been in '29 or maybe '30."

I was so surprised I nearly dropped my hoe. "You knew my grandfather?"

He laughed. "Sure did. Have to tell you about some of

the shenanigans him and me pulled in our younger days."

I couldn't get over it! We'd never known anybody who'd known our older relatives. Now this straight-backed old man was here, announcing he had known my grandfather!

"I . . . I sure would like to hear about it, Mr. Simmons."

"Call me Uncle Dave. Everybody else does. By the way, I cut that tree in two and hauled it off the road. Sorry you been put out with the thing. I told Emmett if he pulled a stunt like that again, I'd peel his hide!"

Debra giggled, and her gray eyes glinted with mischief. "He would, too! He's the only man in Clark County that Daddy's afraid of!"

"He's had better raisin' than to do a stunt like that," Uncle Dave said. "Just you come and see me if there's any more trouble. Now then, you want to go huntin' with me and Debra?"

"What?" I glanced at Debra. She framed the words *Say yes* with her lips. "Well, sure I do. When were you thinking of?"

"When! Shoot, boy, I mean *now!*" He laughed and pulled Debra by the hair. "This gal done pestered me into taking her on a coon hunt. So I brought ol' Jasper along. Heard you had a dog."

My face got red, which made me glad it was getting

dark. Tim was still touching noses with Jasper. "Well, yeah, but—"

"Let's see," Uncle Dave said and stooped to look at the two dogs. After a minute, he held Tim's face and looked into his eyes, then he ran his hands over his body and flanks. He stood up and studied him some more.

I couldn't stand the suspense. "He's . . . well, he's not the fastest dog in the world, Uncle Dave."

He didn't answer right away. When he did, his dark eyes were gleaming. "Fastest dog is a greyhound, Barney, and you know what one of *them* would be worth on a coon hunt? *Nothing!* What counts is *smarts!* Dog's either smart or he's dumb. You can teach him lots of things, but you can't teach him sense. Either he's got it or he hasn't. You ready?"

We ran Jasper and Tim half the night, and the next night, too. From then on, Uncle Dave was just as likely to be standing by the porch about dark as not. Lots of times he would bring Debra with him, but not always. She was better in the woods in lots of ways than most boys. I got to where I could just about keep up with the two of them.

I can't perfectly say how that time was for me—being out in the warm spring woods, a big moon shining down, the sound of the dogs far off sounding like bells. I would sit down on an old dead tree and listen to Uncle

Dave spin yarns about the things he and my grand-father used to do. I learned about coons and dogs. How I lived for those nights!

"Is Tim going to be a good coon dog?" I asked one evening. I'd waited for Uncle Dave to say something about him, but he never had. We were standing under a big oak, listening to the dogs follow a cold trail.

"Yep," he answered right back. "He's got good blood. He'd be good in any case, but I can't tell if he's goin' to be good or *great.* Have to wait and see. He's just learnin'."

"How about . . . how about his limp?"

"Be a better dog on a trail without it, but if he's smart enough, it won't matter. You notice him when he got back after treein' that possum? You see how ashamed of himself he was?"

"He sure was." I laughed. "He looked like he'd been caught in a shameful thing!"

"He *was* caught in a shameful thing," Uncle Dave shot back. "Any *real* coon dog ought to be ashamed of himself for treein' anything but a coon!" He snorted. "You got a dog there that's got to want one thing in this world worse than anything else, and that one thing is to please *you!*"

That kind of talk went on for hours and hours, and I soaked it up! I guess I let my work on our place slide, and Jake and Joe got a little sore about that.

Can anyone tell me why it is that just when things are going good something has to come along and mess it up? Uncle Dave said one time that "everybody has to eat his peck of dirt." I thought I had already had mine, but about two weeks after Uncle Dave and Debra first showed up, I got another dose.

It was on a Friday about five o'clock, when a car drove up to the house. It wasn't the Jeep, so I knew it wasn't Uncle Dave. "I wonder who that could be?" I commented to Jake. We all got up and went outside. When I saw who it was, I nearly passed out!

Coach Littlejohn had just gotten out of his fancy Camaro and was opening the door for Miss Jean. "Oh, no!" Jake groaned. Joe turned pale.

I guess Miss Jean must have thought we acted a little strange when we just stared at her. But then she came up close, and I was suddenly glad to see her, no matter what. "Miss Jean! Hey, it's Miss Jean, you guys!" I shouted. Then we all swarmed her and just about hugged her to pieces!

She finally pulled loose, and there was a wet gleam in her eyes as she said, "My! What a *welcome!* Let me look at you!"

We all went inside, everybody talking at once. It was so good to see her, even if I had a sinking feeling about it. I tried to make some sort of plan while everyone was talking and finally decided what tall tale I would give her.

"I have to be in Dallas for a meeting tomorrow," she was saying, "but Cedarville was so close I just couldn't pass up a chance to see you."

"I met her at school when she came looking for you," Coach said. He kept looking at her out of the corner of his eye. "Just thought I'd bring her out."

Then Miss Jean gave *him* a look, and I could see she hadn't expected to find a guy like Coach Littlejohn in the wilds of Arkansas. He looked a lot like Robert Redford, and he dressed real sharp.

"Yes, it was very nice of Coach to bring me," she said. "He thinks the world of you. But I don't have much time, and I really need to meet Mr. and Mrs. Buck."

"Dad's gone on business . . . ," I said.

"And Ma's sick in bed," Joe finished.

In the first place Coach and everyone else thought we were living with our parents, but Miss Jean was looking for an uncle and an aunt. What saved us was a conversation between Coach and Miss Jean that I wouldn't find out about for a long time. When she had met him at school and asked about "the uncle and aunt of the Buck brothers," Coach had said, "We all thought it was their *parents!*" Miss Jean jumped to a conclusion and said, "Why, it's probably a protective thing. They've lost their parents and are reaching out for some security."

So, my brothers and I were safe. At least for the time

being. I was going to tell her that Mom had gone on a visit to Kentucky.

"I really *must* see one of your relatives," Miss Jean said. "For one thing I have to get a signature on a legal paper. The judge insists, and that's another reason why I came. I'll be very quick, but really I must see someone."

Jake piped up. "Come on, Barney." He grabbed me by the arm, then dragged me out of the room and said, "Let's go see if Aunt Ellen's feeling good enough to see Miss Jean."

As soon as we were in the bedroom, Jake whispered, "You gotta be an aunt, Barney!"

"What?"

"It's the only way! Look, Miss Jean has gotta get that paper signed or we're *dead!* So you hafta get into that bed and be Aunt Ellen." I opened my mouth to argue, but he stopped me. "Look, you get into bed and cover up. We'll put a handkerchief over your head and these sunglasses on you. You can say the light hurts your eyes."

"Jake, Miss Jean isn't blind! She'll see—"

"We'll leave just this candle lit, and you can whisper to her."

"I'm too tall!"

"Scrunch up and we'll mess up this quilt and throw it over the foot of the bed."

"They'll wonder why I don't come back with you!"

"You *do* go back. We say Aunt Ellen is getting ready, and you say you gotta go see about Tim or something. Then you run around the house, sneak in the window, and do your stuff. It'll be easy!"

"Why don't *you* do it then? Why am *I* the one who has to do these nutty things?"

"You got the pretty face, Barney." Jake grinned. "Now let's do it!"

We went back inside, and Jake took over, which was a good thing since I couldn't think straight. "Aunt Ellen is waking up. Give her a chance to get awake and you can go in and see her, Miss Jean."

Jake gave me a dig in the ribs with his elbow, and I said, "Oh, I gotta go feed Tim. Be right back."

I got outside and scrambled around the house. It wasn't hard to get back inside through a window, and I was just able to get under the covers and put on the handkerchief and the sunglasses when the door opened. Miss Jean looked in and said, "May I come in, Mrs. Buck?"

I hoped she couldn't see me any better than I could see her. "Yes, come in, please," I said as softly and weakly as I could.

She tiptoed over and sat down in the chair by my bed. I kept my face turned away and said, "I'm sorry about the light. It hurts my eyes."

"That's quite all right, Mrs. Buck." Suddenly I felt her

pat my shoulder, and I nearly jumped out of bed. "I'm so sorry to hear of your illness. I don't see how you get by this far out, especially with your husband gone so much."

"Oh, it's those wonderful boys!" I said weakly. "They take such good care of me. Especially Barney. And I'll be well soon."

"I certainly hope so. Mrs. Buck, are you satisfied with the boys? Are there any problems you think I ought to know about?"

"Oh, my, no!" I said. "I don't know what Roy and me would do without them boys. They're such a comfort!"

Out of the corner of my eye I saw Miss Jean taking notes, so I continued to give us all a good report. I wish we'd been *half* as good as I made us out to be! Finally I thought it was time for a sick woman to quit. "Only one thing bothers me. What would happen to the boys if they had to leave this place? I mean they've done so *well* here. I think it would be real bad for them if they had to leave."

She patted my shoulder again. "I think we won't have to worry about that, Mrs. Buck. It seems to me that despite the . . . primitive conditions . . ." She stumbled a little, but went on, "It would be in the best interests of the boys to leave them here. Do you think you might sign a paper that I have with me? I know you don't feel well, but if I could get your signature, it would be very easy for me to get the report to the judge."

I partially sat up and signed the paper in a shaky, scratchy hand. Then I gave a moan like I was about played out, and Miss Jean said she hoped I would be better soon. Then she left the room.

I jumped off the bed, shed my disguise, and just barely made it around the house in time to meet her walking into the living room.

"Oh," I said in a surprised voice. "You already talked to Aunt Ellen?"

"Oh, yes. And she signed the paper."

Miss Jean said something about going out to eat, but I thought it was a good time to show her how well we were able to cook. I used up what seemed like a week's supply of food, but it was worth it. I cooked up some steaks we were saving for Sunday and then made some french fries and opened some baked beans. We used some lettuce Debra had brought the day before to make a good salad. We had soda and coffee and, for dessert, a Sara Lee pecan cake. After supper we all pitched in and washed the dishes, then we played Monopoly and Trivial Pursuit until Joe nearly fell over from exhaustion.

"Well, boys, I *must* go!" Miss Jean said, looking at her watch. "It's after eleven and I have to catch a bus to Dallas early in the morning."

"Dallas?" Coach said as if he'd just remembered something. "That reminds me. I have to go see my mother tomorrow."

"Your mother? Where does she live?" Miss Jean asked, sort of smiling.

Coach Littlejohn tried to look innocent. "Hurst, Texas—right outside of Dallas." Then he gave her that look that had charmed half the population of pretty girls in Cedarville. "Would you be persuaded to accept a ride from a stranger?"

Miss Jean just smiled, and from the look on her face I wasn't just sure which one of them had just been maneuvered! They walked out, talking about the stuff they would do the next day.

Miss Jean called to us after Coach closed the car door behind her. "I'll write you, and you keep your letters coming, you hear, boys?"

"That was a close one!" Jake said as they drove off. "But we got the right guy for a brother." He threw his arms around my neck and said, "Oh, Grandma, what big eyes you have!"

"Get away from me, you creep!" I shoved him off. "Wonder who I'll have to be next? I'm so many people now I think I'm going nuts."

Jake came right back. "Maybe you can be an actor. They make a bundle, and I'll be your manager. It'll cost you only 10 percent."

And he would have done it, too, if he could have found a way!

8

The Great Chicken Beak Bet

ALL through May I spent every spare minute with Tim, night and day. He was really getting good! That was what Uncle Dave said. I guessed I was learning a little, too, but there was still a lot left to learn.

We kept Tim on a short rope for a while, but whenever Jasper treed a coon, we turned Tim loose. That dog was smart.

"Look at that Tim dog-tapping that tree! I ain't never seen a young dog do that!" Uncle Dave said.

"What does that mean? Tapping a tree?"

"Why, a coon, he'll climb lots of trees, just messin' around. A dog can't see him too often; so most dogs will just find a tree Mr. Coon's gone up. But if he don't see him, why, he'll tear off lookin' for another trail. But a *smart* dog will really check a tree out—go all around it lookin' for that coon. That's what Tim does, see?"

Yep, I was learning, but not as fast as I wanted to. I guessed I wasn't as smart as Tim. The next day we were following Jasper, and I had Tim on a leash. We were passing by an old redgum tree when all of a sudden Tim pulled me to it and started barking like crazy. I looked up, and right at the top was a coon!

Uncle Dave looked funny. "You see that, Barney?"

"See what?"

"Why, Tim got a coon that Jasper missed. And that Jasper don't *miss*—not once in a blue moon." He looked down at Tim. "I seen lots of dogs, but I can't say as I ever saw one that young quite as good."

Boy, did that make me feel proud, but I kept thinking I was spending too much time with the dogs and Uncle Dave and not enough with my own brothers.

As it turned out, I didn't have to worry. Mr. McPherson, the general science and chemistry teacher, had gotten a government grant, and every day Joe worked with him in a special lab. Mr. McPherson told me more than once that Joe was a genius at science.

As for Jake, well, he was on Coach's softball team at church, so he and Coach spent a lot of time together. "Coach is writing letters to Miss Jean," he told me.

"I don't like *that.* I want to keep her in the dark as much as we can. What if he tells her something?"

"I bet he's got her so dizzy she doesn't know right from left. You know how women are."

Anyway, Jake stayed busy, but the one thing he did that made a lot of noise was the chicken beak bet.

Junior Pote's family kept some chicken houses. Which wouldn't have meant a whole lot except that Junior's little brother Alfred was on the same softball team with Jake. They got along pretty well. I think Alfred was a lot better kid than his older brother.

Anyway, one time before a game, Alfred had taken Jake home with him for lunch and had shown him the chicken houses.

"I never knew there were so many chickens in the world, Barney," Jake told me later. "All packed together and hardly room to step. But the thing you won't believe is the way they cut their beaks off."

"The way they do *what?"*

"That's right, they do that. They take these little bitty chickens and cut their beaks off. Not with a knife—there's this red-hot wire—and they pick up a little chicken and just cut his beak off with that wire."

"I don't believe that, Jake!"

"I'm not kidding, Barney. I couldn't believe it myself."

"Sounds like a bunch of cruds to me. Why do they do it?"

"I asked Alfred, and he said chickens go wild when they see blood. When they get a little older, if one of the chickens gets a scratch—just a tiny bit of blood—all the other chickens will go for him and just peck him to death. So they cut their beaks off to keep 'em from hurting each other."

"Well, it sounds wrong to me." I rubbed Tim's silky ears. "I think people who do that are cruel."

"I think you're right," Jake agreed, but I could tell he was thinking. I hated it when Jake did that; it generally meant I was going to get into trouble.

And it did.

The next week Uncle Dave and I came in from a run with Tim and Jasper. When we were getting a drink, Uncle Dave asked me, "What's this about a bet Jake has with the Potes?"

"What? I don't know anything about it."

"You're always the last to hear, ain't you, Barney?" He sat down. "Way I hear it, your brother's got a crazy bet with old man Pote about chickens."

"Why, Jake doesn't have any money—and he doesn't know anything about chickens."

"I hope you're wrong about that, Barney. Folks around here expect a fellow to stand by his word and his bet."

"But—he's just a kid."

Uncle Dave grinned at me. "I don't think he is. I think

he's a midget. Never saw 'just a kid' operate like that boy. Seen a few bank robbers and one or two con artists do it—but this young feller, he's got 'em all beat."

"What was the bet?" I was afraid to ask, but I had to know.

"Well, it seems that about two hundred chickens used to get pecked to death in a house before they started debeaking them. Now they have to hire someone to do that, and it costs a pretty penny. The chicken farmers would be happy to cut it out. Jake says if they'll let him have a go at it, he'll guarantee that no chicken'll be pecked to death and none'll be debeaked. So, the way the bet is, if all the chickens live without being debeaked, Jake gets two hundred dollars and Silas pays for whatever Jake did to win the bet. For each one that is pecked to death, Jake pays Silas Pote one dollar."

"But—that could cost Jake two hundred dollars!"

"Maybe more. He better know *something,* Barney," he said as he got up and left.

I nabbed Jake later that day. When I started in on him, he just gave me his *superior* smile.

"I'll handle it, Barney. It's a lead-pipe cinch." Nothing I said could shake him.

"Well, don't come crying to me when you lose. We don't have the money to pay for dead chickens."

I kept thinking about that payment more and more. We didn't have a dollar saved. The watermelons weren't ripe yet, but they were looking good. I kept on trying to count them. If nothing went wrong, we would have enough to pay off the note; but I still worried.

One morning Jake said, "Barney, we got to work on the chickens today. All of us."

"Not *me!* And not Joe, either. You got yourself into this. Now just haul yourself out!"

"I've got to have a little help, and it's two hundred dollars clear money almost. Nearly a fifth of that note, right?"

Jake knew how to hit me where it hurt. He knew how I worried about the money. I finally gritted my teeth. "All right, Jake, you little thug! What's the plan this time?"

He explained it in less than five minutes, and Joe was thrilled. I thought it was by far the most insane of all Jake's schemes—which was really saying a lot! But I had to go along with it.

We went over to the Pote place around nine o'clock. "Why don'tcha just give us the money now and save yourselves a lot of work?" Junior asked. All the Potes were grinning like crazy.

Jake didn't even say hello. "Remember, we get the chicks all day with nobody around to bother us."

"Take two days if you want," Mr. Pote said. "Go right ahead." There was a big laugh as we went in.

"I think they're gonna *pray* over them chickens, Pa. That's so they'll turn the other cheek," Junior said.

We Bucks started in and put Jake's "plan" into action. By eleven-thirty we were through.

"Scatter some of this around, will you?" Jake said, handing us some shreds of moss he'd brought in a big sack. "Just to throw 'em off the scent." He also insisted we make a little *X* with a purple Magic Marker on top of every chick's head.

We went to the door and told the Potes to come in. They looked around. Mr. Pote spotted an *X* on top of one chick, then noticed one on each of the others. "You put a hex on these here chicks, boy?" Mr. Pote roared with laughter.

Junior found some of the moss and sniffed at it. "It'll take more than moss to keep these chickens sweet!"

As we left, Jake said, "I'll come back twice more for the rest of the treatment." Then we marched off. The Potes were laughing like crazy, and by nightfall the Bucks of Goober Holler had the reputation of being not only crazy dog thieves, but witch doctors as well.

Those chickens grew up fast. Cedarville was watching that house the way some communities do a World Series. People who raised chickens laughed the loudest—and there were a lot of them. All the same, they kept a close watch, just in case. The bet was to be settled by the second of July. If any chickens ended up dead, it would happen by then.

We got a scare once because there was a dead

chicken in the house, but old man Pote was a good man. He knew his chickens and decided that this one had died of heat, so he didn't count it. There were several like that, but not one had been pecked to death.

It was interesting the way some people began saying howdy to us. One day Debra told me, "See, if you would just be a little more open, folks would like you fine, like I do." Then she clammed up as if she'd said too much and went off with her nose in the air.

Just like a girl.

9

The Great Catapult Caper

I was pulling seed ticks off Tim one afternoon in mid-June when Joe and Jake came in from the woods. Jake didn't waste any time. "Barney, how'd you like to raise enough money to pay off that old man Simmons *right now?"*

I just looked at him and went back to picking ticks. "My younger brother Jake is taking care of all that. I'm surprised you haven't heard about him—the Watermelon King of the South?"

Jake got a little huffy, but it didn't faze him for long. Nothing ever did. "Sure, but we need a back-up system, and Joe and I have come up with just the thing."

"Joe?"

"Well, actually it's his idea, but I'm promoting it."

"You mean he does the work and you take the money!"

"That's the kind of rotten thing you say sometimes, Barney!" Jake said. "Here I go to all the trouble to set up this surefire plan, and all you can do is act smart and criticize!"

I removed the last of the ticks and stood up. "Well, let's go see what you've got. It can't be as nutty as some of your other stunts."

Was I ever wrong about *that!*

They took me to the Caddo River, which is only about a mile from our place. They'd found a wide part, maybe thirty-five feet, just below a high bluff that stuck out over the water. The river was pretty deep and swift.

"We have to go up on that bluff," Jake said. So we went scrambling up the steep sides to the top. When we got there, Jake waved his hand and said proudly, "There she is!"

I took a look and said, "Yeah, but *what* is she?"

"It's a *catapult,* for crying out loud!" Jake said with that superior look he sometimes had. "Don't you know anything, Barney?"

"You didn't know what it was either, Jake, until I told you." Joe grinned. "I saw this in an old movie on TV, Barney. It was about the old days when they were first starting to have airplanes on ships. Well, they got them off the deck with a thing like this, and they called it a catapult."

Joe and Jake had built a track out of old odds and ends of lumber that must have been at least thirty feet long or more. I hated to think how much work they must have put into the thing! Right at the edge of the bluff were two pine trees about ten feet apart. There was rope of some kind on the ground, and each tree had one end of the rope tied about a foot up on the trunk. I went over and picked up the rope.

"Why—this rope is made of *rubber!"* I said in surprise.

"Yeah, I got it from that old warehouse out by the sale barn," Jake said. "The guy said it was reject surgical tubing, and boy, does it ever stretch!"

I tried it and it really did. "What . . . what does this thing *do?"*

"Look here, Barney," Joe said and began pointing at the thing. "You put this rubber cable over the hook that's on this piece of cable like this. . . ." He had a heavy sisal rope that ran right down the middle of the track and was fastened to some sort of contraption at the far end. "Come on and I'll show you how the gears work." At the end was a kind of homebuilt winch. He had a drum made out of an old barrel, and a gear made of wood was fastened to it. On the other side was a handle to turn the thing around. "See, when I turn the handle, the drum turns and it pulls the cables real tight."

I watched as he turned it, and every time it moved, the teeth went into a sprocket and locked it tight so it couldn't slip back. Then the ropes got tighter. "Hey, the whole thing's like a gigantic slingshot!" I exclaimed.

Joe grinned. "Sure, that's what a catapult is." He kept rolling it around, and pretty soon the rubber cables were even with a flat wooden thing in the middle of the track. Joe took one more turn, slipped the rubber cable into a hook under the bottom of the flat part, and then eased the sisal rope.

I pulled at the cable and it was as tight as steel. I looked at Joe's invention. "Wait a minute—this flat thing. When you pull the trigger, it shoots this flat thing out over the bluff and it falls in the river—right?"

"Not *exactly,"* Jake said. "We call this part the 'craft.' . . ." Joe gave him a dig with his elbow. "I mean we call it the *Enterprise.* But it doesn't go into the launch. See this little rope? Well, it catches the *Enterprise* when it gets about twenty feet into space. Otherwise, we might lose it in the river." He looked a little nervous, cleared his throat, and said, "The . . . ah, *pilot* is who actually gets launched."

I couldn't believe my ears. Walking to the edge of the bluff, I stared down at the river. It looked more like a hundred feet away than thirty. I walked back and gave the cable a pluck, and it sang like a guitar string. Then I looked at my idiot brothers and shook my head.

"Who do you think would be crazy enough to let himself be shot out of this thing like a rock out of a sling-shot? Of course, he might not drown in the river—he might be lucky enough to get his neck broken before he got the chance!" They were both looking at me, and I suddenly realized why. "Oh, no! No way! You think that maybe *I* would be such a crazy?"

"Yes, because you're the oldest and the biggest." Jake had the nasty habit of throwing that up to me whenever there was a dirty job to be done. Then when something good was on tap, it was, "You ought to let Joe and me have it because we're the youngest and the smallest."

"I see. And what makes me want to do this nutty thing?"

"Because it's worth a *fortune,"* Jake answered. "Look, I know it may be a *little* risky, but that's exactly what's going to make it work! You know how kids are, Barney. Like at the fair, they all want to ride the hairiest ride to show off. They want the girls to see them and start that silly female squealing like they do. And they want to show the other kids they're not chicken. So they all have to do it, don't you know?"

Jake was right about that. I'd noticed it myself lots of times at the fair. "So the plan is to charge the kids money to risk their necks on this thing?"

"They'll do it, too!" Jake insisted. "But somebody has to go first and show them they won't get killed or some-thing."

"I won't do it!" I said. And I meant it. At first. But after about an hour of steady argument, Jake wore me down. That note was coming due, and we needed every penny we could dig up. So I found myself agreeing to it.

Actually, I wasn't too worried. I never had been afraid of heights and I could swim pretty well. Besides, I found out that I even had some sort of need to prove I was tough!

Anyway, I peeled off my clothes and lay down on the deck of the *Enterprise.* Joe had made little holes in the front for me to hang on to, and there was a cleat in the back to hook my toes over. I got a good grip and said, "Let her go!"

The catapult fired when you knocked a peg out of the piece that held it to the rear of the track. I heard a *thump* when Joe hit it, and off I went.

It took only one quick second and everything blurred! It was a lot like the bottom part of a roller coaster when the force pushed you against the back of your seat—only now the pressure was on my legs and hands. Everything flashed by and I nearly lost my grip. Then I was out over the edge, the river far below. The rope caught the *Enterprise,* which scraped my chest and legs as I slid off and began my free flight.

I'd planned to stick my arms out in front of me and do a Superman number, but it didn't work like that. Somehow the force threw my legs up, and the first thing I knew I was doing a somersault! The earth went around then, and it was *fun!*

Anyway, around and around I went, right toward the water, with no idea if I would hit headfirst or feetfirst. Actually I did a wild kind of belly flop, but it really didn't hurt. It was no problem to swim out and greet Jake and Joe, who had scrambled down to meet me.

"That was *great!*" Jake shouted.

I wiped the water from my eyes. "Well, it's really not bad." Then I felt something like bees stinging my chest and legs. I looked down and there were little splinters all over my front.

"What in . . . ," I said. Then it *really* started to hurt! "Why didn't you get that thing *smooth?*" I squealed, giving Jake a furious glare. "I could wring your neck!"

I grabbed my clothes and headed back to the house. The pain got worse and worse. "I'll get you for this!" I raved all the way home. Then to make things just perfect, Uncle Dave and Debra were on the porch, waiting to go hunting.

Debra took one look at me and ran to meet us. "Barney! What's *wrong?*" she screamed.

"These two idiots have killed me!"

"Let's have a look, boy," Uncle Dave said. We went inside to the kitchen, and I took off my shirt. "My land! I never seen one boy get so many splinters—and in such a funny place! You got any more?"

"They're all down my legs, too, and they're killing me!"

"Well, they gotta come out. Put some shorts or something on and we'll get at it. Can't leave 'em in to fester." I excused myself to put on some cutoffs. "You got any tweezers?" he asked when I returned.

"No, but I got some little needle-nose pliers," Joe said. He ran to his toolbox and was back in a flash.

"All right, hold still," Uncle Dave said. Then he gave a jerk, which nearly knocked me off the table. "Be still there," he said with a grin. "Feller has fun, he's gotta be willing to pay for it."

"Fun?!" I shouted. "I don't see any fun—"

"You just quiet down," he said, and his eyes got a little hard. "Them splinters gotta come out—all of 'em. You wanna be a man about it or not?"

Put that way, what could I do? I lay down on the table and clamped my lips together. I'd show him Jake wasn't the only one in the family with Indian in him!

Uncle Dave was as careful as he could be, but I was ready to quit long before he was. Finally he got all the big ones and said, "My eyes ain't no good for this close work. One of you boys wanna get the little ones?"

"Don't let those monsters near me," I said. "I'll do it!"

"You can't," he said. "You can't even reach some of 'em. Here, Debra, you get these little ones."

She took the pliers and began working on the small

ones. I was mortified. Here I was, stripped down to my skinny old frame, poked full of splinters like a porcupine—and a *girl* picking at me!

She was real quick and easy. I'll say that much. Finally she said, "I guess that's all. Do you have any alcohol?"

"Sure we do," Jake said. He jumped up and got the rubbing alcohol and handed it to her.

"This'll burn," she said. When she touched me with it, I just about went through the roof. But Uncle Dave was watching and so were my brothers, so I acted cool, as if it were water. She was very careful, and when she was through, she stepped back. Her hands were trembling. "I didn't mean to hurt you, Barney."

"Didn't hurt that much," I said as tough as I could. I put on my shirt, somehow managing not to scream. "Let's go hunting."

"I guess you've had about enough excitement for one day." Uncle Dave grinned. "You take it easy and tell how you ended up in this condition."

By that time Jake and Joe had fixed something for us all to eat. After we got through telling about the catapult, Uncle Dave was laughing until he had tears in his eyes. He whooped and hollered and stomped the floor until I got a little irritated. Debra was no help. She got the giggles, too.

"It wasn't that funny!" I finally said.

Uncle Dave wiped at his eyes. "Well, I'm sorry, Barney, but I tell you it took me back to your granddad. I guess Jake here is bred right back to him. It's just the sort of stunt old Ed would pull!" Then before we sat down and ate, he told us about some of the capers Granddad had done.

It was pretty late when they got up from the table. Before they left, Uncle Dave asked, "You see any strange-looking folks hanging around here, boys?"

"Well, yeah, a few times we've seen a man. Never very clear, though. Why?"

He looked right at me and said, "There's a lot of talk about you folks. You know about all the dogs that's been stolen. Well, most of them have been taken in this general area, close to Goober Holler. Some folks are saying you Bucks are mixed up in it."

"But that's not true!" I said. "Why don't they come and ask us?"

"Barney," Debra said, "you haven't been too easy to see."

I knew she was right.

"Maybe if you'd just be a little more friendly toward people . . ." Her voice trailed off at the look on my face.

I couldn't say a word. She just didn't understand. "I don't guess we'll do that," I said finally. "People will just have to think what they want."

"I expect you'll get a visit from the sheriff pretty soon," Uncle Dave said just as he stepped out the door. He turned and saw the grim look on my face. "Don't fret about it. It won't come to nothin'. Thing is, lots of folks have been talkin' about the Bucks of Goober Holler, and Jed Tanner's up for re-election. He's gotta make some sort of trip out here just so he can say he was here. Matter of fact, you ought to keep your eyes open for that stranger you seen a few times. Might be worth lookin' into."

Just what I needed. Something else to worry about. But there wasn't anything I could do about it all, so I just did my best to not think about it.

About two days later Sheriff Tanner did make a visit, and he had lots of questions. I told him my dad would drop in to see him as soon as he got home.

I called Clyde collect, and he said that he was due to come through Cedarville the following Thursday on the way to a big auction in Baton Rouge. When he arrived, both of us went to Sheriff Tanner's office.

The sheriff was a sharp-eyed man, about forty years old. He had a way about him that made me nervous, almost like he was looking right inside my head instead of listening to what I was saying. I let Clyde do most of the talking.

"Like I say, Shuruf Tanner, I'm a travelin' man, and my wife's poorly and has to stay with her folks in

Kentucky quite a bit. But my boys, why, they're downright trustworthy!"

Sheriff Tanner didn't say much. He just gave Clyde a hard look. Finally he said, "You leave these boys alone too much, Buck."

Clyde got a little nervous. "Well, that's a fact, Shuruf. Nobody hates it worse than me, but a man's gotta make a livin', now don't he?"

The sheriff stared at Clyde a long time, then nodded slowly. "Sure, but it seems hard leaving those boys alone for such long periods. Maybe you ought to find another line of work."

Clyde nodded. "*Exactly* what I'm aiming to do, Shuruf Tanner!" He kept on talking, but I could see that the sheriff wasn't one to be taken in by talk. We left as soon as we could. Outside Clyde mopped his brow. "Whew! That lawman won't be an easy man to keep foolin'!"

Clyde stayed around for a week that time, and we had fun fishing and running the dog. As for the catapult, it went great! We had smoothed it down until it was like silk and put a coat of polyurethane on it just to be sure. We practiced and worked on the thing all the time until I could do the stunt easily. And we checked out the river real carefullike to make sure nobody would get washed away.

Before long, we had our "grand opening." It worked just as Jake had predicted. Just about every kid in the county came out for it. They had to show how tough they were—especially since *I* had gone off the fool thing and I was nothing but a city slicker. Our little enterprise went great for the first two weeks we were out of school. We let kids ride only during the afternoon, except on Sunday when we shut down, and charged a quarter a launch. We wound up making twenty to thirty dollars a day.

By the end of the second week we had an even two hundred dollars, and we were just getting started! More kids heard about the ride and started coming over. Jake was bigheaded about it all. He swaggered around, letting everyone know it was his idea.

Then it happened. I shoulda known it would. Something *always* happens.

Billy Fairly was going up in the air and somehow bent his arm under him and broke it when he hit the water. We got him to a doctor and it was a real mess. His folks threatened to have us arrested.

Sheriff Tanner came out the next day. I told him Dad was gone. "I really came out to see you boys. You'll have to take that fool slingshot thing down. It ain't safe. Somebody's gonna get killed sooner or later."

There was no arguing with him. "All right, Sheriff," I said.

He turned to go, then stopped. "By the way, you'll have to pay the Fairly boy's doctor bill. I brought it with me."

He handed me a piece of paper. My heart sank: $236.55. That was thirty-six dollars and fifty-five cents *more* than we'd made.

I showed it to Jake, and he stared at it for a long time. "Well, back to the old drawing board!" was all he could say.

10
Two Grand Finales

JAKE, how're those chickens doing?" I asked the day after we dismantled the catapult. "That bet's almost over, isn't it?"

"Yeah, Barney. In fact, the day after next we go over to old man Pote's and get the money."

"I sure hope you're right, Jake," I muttered.

The day of reckoning arrived. On the second of July, Uncle Dave and Debra came over and drove us to the Potes. Jake had been back there three or four times, mostly to see Alfred, but had always done something nutty in the chicken house. One time he brought along some sulfur and closed himself in. He buried it in the ground, but they didn't know that. Another time he had five gallons of kerosene that he dumped. Just crazy stuff.

When we pulled into their driveway, I nearly fell out of the Jeep. Three hundred people must have been there! It looked like everybody who raised chickens in the county—plus their families *and* the usual bunch of curiosity seekers—were gathered around. I saw Emmett Simmons and the sheriff talking and looking at us. Even most of our teachers were there.

I leaned over and whispered to Jake, "Oh, good job, genius. We're trying to stay hid, and now everybody and his brother has his eyes on us." We climbed out of the Jeep, and Mr. Pote called us over to the door of the chicken house. "Folks, I want you to know that this bet was made fair and square. I thought this here boy was crazy when he done it, but there's been not one chicken dead from peckin' in this house—and every chicken has a beak!"

A little murmur went up through the crowd. Mr. Pote pulled his billfold out and counted out the two hundred dollars. "Son," he said, handing Jake the money, "it wasn't in the bet that you have to tell how you done it, but I sure would like to know."

Several of the men were nodding, and Jake spoke right up. "I don't mind telling you, Mr. Pote, but I want to remind you of one thing, right here in the sheriff's presence . . ." A little laugh went up, and Jake continued. "I *never* claimed that the way to keep chickens from pecking each other to death without cutting their beaks off was something you would *want* to do, did I?"

Mr. Pote nodded. "Now that's a fact, boy. And no shame to you no matter what you done. Mostly I'm just curious."

"Well, all right, I'll show you. Barney, will you bring me one of those chickens. Any one of 'em."

I went inside and grabbed the first one I saw. They had really grown since we'd been there to doctor them up! I brought it out and gave it to Jake.

"Mr. Pote, you wanna lean in real close and watch what I'm doing?" Jake asked.

Mr. Pote leaned down and watched as Jake held the chicken under one arm and kept the head still with his hand. Then he took his fingernail and touched the chicken's eye. "There it is!" he said.

Mr. Pote squinted as Jake held up a shiny plastic lens. "What in tarnation is that thing?" he asked in bewilderment.

"It's a chicken contact lens," Jake said with a grin. A hum went around the crowd, and Jake raised his voice to be heard. "You know how people use them instead of glasses. Well, I read that a chicken ranch in Birmingham, Alabama, was trying to get out of debeaking. There was a picture and article about it in the newspaper about six months ago. I ordered enough of these to do this house."

"But how does it work?" Mr. Pote asked, still peering at the bit of plastic.

"The paper said the plastic cuts out the red color so the chickens never see any blood."

"And every one of my chickens has these things on their eyes?"

"Oh, sure, we had to do that."

Another hum went around. Then Mr. Pote looked straight at Jake. "How much they gonna cost me?"

Jake suddenly grinned at him and said simply, "Not more than twice what it cost you to get them debeaked, Mr. Pote."

Several groans went up. Someone said, "Why, that smart-aleck kid—"

Mr. Pote just held up his hand. When it was quiet, he said, "What are you mad about? I'm the one who lost the bet. And since I been wearing long pants, I always figured if somebody could get the best of me in a trade or a bet, he was welcome to the end of it. Young feller, you done me." He looked a little rueful. "Sure do hate to think what will happen when you're grown and turned loose on this unsuspecting world—but anyhow here's my hand."

That was the end of it. We got home as fast as we could. Jake handed me the two hundred dollars.

"Barney, I'm sure glad one thing I did was right."

I put my arm around him and the other around Joe. We didn't hug much, but I was feeling pretty proud of my brothers that night. "You always do one thing right, Jake," I said, "and that's just being my brother."

He was a little embarrassed at being hugged, so I let him go. "Now then, we're ready for the great watermelon sale! I bet we get the rest of that old note money in a month!"

The Fourth of July was just a couple days away, and the watermelons had been swelling up so fast we could almost see them grow. Uncle Dave had said, "That always was the best watermelon ground in the county. Lots of prizewinning melons out of that patch."

Uncle Dave drove over to invite us all on a coon hunt the day Jake had settled the chicken beak bet. Debra was with him as usual. I noticed Bubba in the backseat looking disgusted.

We were in the front of the house, and Uncle Dave wouldn't take no for an answer.

"You have to run Tim with a pack, Barney. He'll learn a lot from that, and you'll learn something, too. Now we'll meet over at the Dale place about seven tonight. You bring Jake and Joe with you. We'll have six to seven dogs, and we'll make a night of it."

"Well, I guess we'll be there." I watched them pull out

and tried to think of some way to get out of it. But Uncle Dave was right, and I knew it.

We met the bunch there, and Tim seemed to be in his element. Bubba didn't say anything, but he sneered every time he looked at Tim. He said something about a "crippled mutt" to another coon hunter, Todd Reynolds.

But I didn't let that comment spoil the night for me. I was ready to have some fun, especially since I'd gotten pretty good at getting through the woods. Hunting was one time when my long legs were an asset.

We ran Tim and Jasper until late. The high point came when the dogs had followed something for nearly two hours, and we'd tried to catch up. Jake said they were after a deer; Joe thought it was maybe a fox. I didn't say anything, but kept my eyes on Uncle Dave.

One by one, all the dogs came back with their tongues hanging out like red neckties. Finally they were all in but Tim. I felt bad, thinking he must have given up and gone back to the house.

"I knew that three-legged mutt would fade," Bubba sneered. We all sat down around the fire, and I felt pretty low. Debra sat down close to me. I felt better when she gave me a smile, but then Bubba started telling a story about some dog that wasn't even worth killing, and I knew he was making it up to shame Tim and me.

All of a sudden Uncle Dave said, "Shut up, Bubba!"

Then he held his head up high, listening hard. "Let's go get that coon!" Uncle Dave said.

"What coon?" Bubba asked in surprise.

"The one Tim's got treed and won't let go of." Uncle Dave ran out into the dark, and we all got up and followed him. As we ran, I heard a bark. It was Tim!

We ran until we came to a stand of white oak. Tim was dancing around under one of them, baying in a deep voice.

Uncle Dave flashed his light up into the tree. "There he is! A big one."

"How'd the other dogs miss that one?" Debra asked. "They were all together, weren't they?"

Uncle Dave turned around, a big smile on his bearded face. "Sure they were, but some dogs are smarter than others. What probably happened is time. Tim marked the tree."

"What does that mean?" I asked.

"It means coons aren't stupid," Uncle Dave replied. "There was a coon all right, but he fooled 'em by climbin' out to the end of a limb and gettin' into the next tree. Then while the dogs were yappin' at the tree he went up, he came down on another tree. Only his plan didn't work, 'cause there was a dog out there that's smarter than him. *And* smarter than the rest of the dogs." He reached down and gave Tim a big slap on the side. "Tim marked the tree! He knew the raccoon went up the first tree, but wasn't there no more, so he figured the critter musta gone to another tree. So he started circlin' and checkin' all the trees and he found Mr. Coon maybe just comin' down. Mr. Tim, he got that coon back where he belongs."

"Ain't no dog that smart," one of the men grumbled.

"Not many, not very many," Uncle Dave said slowly. "I been coon huntin' for nearly sixty years, and I seen maybe three or four coon dogs that were really smart."

"You're saying that dog is one of the smartest you ever saw, Granddad?" Bubba asked. He was staring at Tim with an angry look on his face.

Uncle Dave just pointed up at the tree. "There's your proof."

Finally we got back to the house and thanked Uncle Dave. I was feeling better than I maybe should have, but I had *some dog!*

Jake and Joe went right to bed. I was pretty tired, but too excited to sleep. I was just sitting on the porch watching for the sun to come up when suddenly Tim jumped up. He made a growling sound I'd never heard—a mean sound from way down in his chest. Then, without warning, he jumped off the porch and ran to the melon patch. I gave a yell and went after him. Just as I got there, the dark form of a man rose up, and Tim went right for him.

Whoever it was let out a yell and went down as Tim

hit him broadside. I was so scared my knees turned to water. Then Tim gave a yelp as if something had hurt him, so I plowed right in. The man was getting up, and I tackled him around the knees just right, which made him go down again with all of us tangled up—me and him and Tim.

I began hollering and Tim was baying as if he had treed a coon and the stranger was snorting and cursing. He was tall and so strong that I couldn't believe it. He grabbed me with one hand and threw me off so hard you'd think I was stuffed with feathers. Then he did the same thing to Tim. The man jumped to his feet and made for the tree line. Tim would have gone after him, but I grabbed him and held on, still hollering.

A light had come on in the house, and Jake and Joe came running out in their pajamas. "What's going on?" Jake was shouting.

"Somebody was out here and we jumped him," I said.

"I bet it was the same one I saw," Joe said. "Where is he?"

"He ran off that way." I pointed to the trees. "Tim flushed him out."

"What do you think he was doing here?" Jake asked.

"I dunno, maybe he was here to steal Tim. He may be the one who's stealing all the dogs around here," I replied.

"We better get our guns and keep guard," Jake said, his eyes bright with excitement.

"No, he won't be back. It's almost dawn." Just then I stepped on something sharp with my bare foot. I picked it up and looked at it. "Look at this. He must have dropped it."

"It's a hypodermic needle," Joe said. "We use them in experiments at that special school lab all the time."

"I know," Jake said. "He was going to drug Tim! That way he would keep him quiet."

"Maybe he's one of those drug addicts," Joe said.

"We better give this to the sheriff," I said. "Maybe it has fingerprints on it." We went back to the house, but there was no sleep for any of us then. I planned on taking the needle to the sheriff but figured there was no hurry.

The next evening, Coach Littlejohn came out in his old pickup. "You fellas got any watermelons you want to sell?" he said with a grin. He knew we were banking heavily on that patch to make some money, and I figured he just wanted to buy one for himself.

"Sure, Coach," I said. "I'll pick you a real good one."

He snapped his fingers. "One? I want twenty!" He grinned. "We're having a picnic at the church tomorrow, and what could be better refreshments than good watermelons? If I get them in the coolers tonight, they'll be cold by tomorrow. We'll pay three bucks apiece."

"Why, that's sixty bucks!" Jake said.

"Early ones are always more," Coach said. "'Course I got to test one to see if they're good."

"We can handle that." We went to the porch and picked out a big, plump melon and broke it right there. It was as red as the inside of Tim's mouth. When we tasted it, it was sweet as honey and firm as anyone could want.

"Hey, couldn't be better than this!" Coach said. "Let's get twenty more like this one."

In no time at all we loaded up his pickup, and he was on his way to cool them off. "Boy! Sixty bucks!" Jake said. "And we got a patch full just like that, Barney."

"I guess you were right about this scheme, Jake," I said.

"That's two winners in a row." He grinned at me. "I'm on a roll."

I guess we all got a little silly then. I know I'd been worried sick about the note; Jake and Joe must have been thinking about it more than they had let on, too. We hollered and wrestled and made crazy jokes until after eleven. When we got up the next morning, we were still pretty happy.

Since we weren't going to the Fourth of July picnic, I planned on reading all day, and Jake and Joe decided at the last minute to hitch a ride in and see a movie. That left me alone all afternoon.

It must have been about two o'clock when I heard

somebody coming down our road. I looked up. Uncle Dave and Debra were coming toward the house. He let her out of the Jeep, then drove back down the road in a hurry. Debra walked over to the porch to meet me. *Boy, is she getting pretty,* I thought to myself.

"Hi, Barney." She smiled. "You all by yourself today?"

"Sure am. Jake and Joe went to take in a movie."

"Let's go for a walk, OK?"

"Sure." I walked with her down the trail to the pond, where we'd fished a couple of times.

Debra seemed a little strange. "Something wrong, Debra?" I asked.

She picked up a stick and poked at the dragonflies hovering over the weeds close to the bank. Then she threw the stick into the pond and turned around. "You're getting taller," she said, her eyes still on me.

Then I got nervous! I'd gotten so used to her I had just about learned to forget she was a girl. But that was pretty hard to do when she was standing so close that I could smell whatever it was that made her smell so good. Her skin had a glow, and she had thick lashes and a sort of heavy-lidded look that bothered me when she turned her gaze right at me. I don't know . . . it just made me feel like mush.

"Barney," she said, putting her hand on my arm, "I want to tell you something."

"Well, what is it?" I had kept so many lies going I just didn't know which one had caught up with me.

"I hope you won't be mad at me. Last week I heard Daddy talking to Mr. Hargrave, his lawyer. They didn't know I could hear, but I could." She hesitated a minute. "Daddy got to talking about people who owe him money, and he was telling Mr. Hargrave what to do about them." She squeezed my arm, and I almost jumped into the pond. "He said you had to make a thousand-dollar payment or lose your place."

"Well, I guess it's no big secret. Of course, you don't have to tell anyone else."

"No, I won't." She moved a little closer so that her arm was actually touching me. Her breath smelled real sweet. "But can you pay it, Barney? Does your dad have the money?"

"Well, to tell you the truth, it's going to be close." My voice was doing funny things, and I cleared my throat and went on. "If we do as well with these watermelons as it looks like, though, we'll be able to handle it."

Then she whispered. "Barney, *I've* got some money. Nearly three hundred dollars all my own. I want you to promise me you'll take it as a loan, if you need it."

"Gee, Debra, that's swell of you, but if the watermelons—"

Suddenly Debra threw her arms around me, pulled my head down, and gave me the hardest kiss I ever had. I stood there thinking how red my face must be getting. Then she said, "Remember, Barney, no matter what happens, I'll stand by you." She turned and walked toward the road. I nearly fell over Tim, who gave a bark of complaint when I accidentally kicked his side.

"What in the name of common sense was *that* all about?" I said out loud, staring at the road.

Then I saw a pickup. It was Coach Littlejohn's. From the look on his face, we had trouble. Sure enough, when he pulled up and got out, the first words out of his mouth were: "Barney, I hate to tell you this, but you've got problems!"

"What's the matter?"

He got out and went to the back of the truck. "Smell this," he said, picking up a piece of watermelon.

I didn't have to get close. It smelled awful. "What happened to it, Coach?" I walked to the back of the pickup. There was a pile of melons—about as many as he had taken.

"I took them to the picnic and the first one was fine," he said slowly. "Everyone was saying how it was the finest melon they'd had in years. Then we cut the second one, and it smelled like this." His face told me how he was feeling. "Well, we cut them all, Barney, and sixteen of the twenty were bad. I don't know what it is. Nobody ever saw anything like it."

Suddenly I knew. "Wait a minute, Coach. I'll be right back." I ran into the house and picked up the hypodermic needle, then took it to him. "Last night Tim and I caught a man in the watermelon patch. I thought he was the dog thief and that the needle was for Tim. Now I don't think so."

Coach Littlejohn lifted it and smelled the tip. "This is it, I'm afraid, Barney. Same smell. You say he dropped this?"

"Yes. We'd all been gone on a coon hunt. He must have known we were gone. Tim would have nailed him sooner."

"I'll have the sheriff look at this. Maybe Mr. McPherson can tell us what it is."

"What difference does it make? We can't sell the melons. He must've given all of them he could a shot. But we can't know which are good and which are bad without cutting them open."

Coach must have known how terrible I felt, because he put his arm around me. "Barney, I wish I could help. It's not the end of the world, although I know it must seem like it right now." He tightened his grip. "Remember what we read about Joseph in Sunday school last week? How when he got sent to jail, everything must have seemed pretty bleak."

"I remember, Coach," I said with the best smile I could muster. "And you said God was working in

Joseph's life, getting him in a position to save his brothers from the coming famine."

Coach Littlejohn didn't answer for a moment. He was looking at me in a funny way. I got a little restless. Coach had never talked to me directly about religion. Of course, in Sunday school class he'd let me know how he stood. But now we were alone, and I knew he was trying to tell me something. "Barney," he said finally, "are you *sure* there isn't something you want to tell me?"

Uncle Dave said that if you throw a rock at a pack of dogs, the only one that'll holler is the one you hit! And I was hit! "What . . . what do you mean, Coach?"

"I mean, you've got people here who care about you, and that's more than money in the bank, but I know you have secrets, Barney."

He didn't say anything else, but his eyes were too direct for me to meet. It was a wonder he hadn't asked before, considering the crazy way we'd been living. But I knew one thing for sure: Coach was a friend if I ever had one.

Right then, I wanted more than anything else in the world to spill the whole thing, but it wasn't just *my* life. I had Jake and Joe to think about. "Coach, I guess you know that, well, things aren't normal for me. And I know you'd like to help, but there just isn't anything you can do!"

He looked at me. "Barney, I've been trying to tell

you—in Sunday school class—that there's one person who's always ready to help and that's Jesus Christ. I don't want to force anything on you, but let me say that if you have anything that's too heavy to carry, why, that's exactly what that verse meant that I talked about last week. 'Come all ye that labor and are heavy laden and I will give you rest.'"

It got real quiet, and I just stood there thinking about how good it would be just to unload all the stuff that had piled up on me. Coach Littlejohn was waiting, but I guess he saw I wasn't ready—not just then.

He looked at me with a funny smile. "It's going to be tough, isn't it, Barney?"

"Sure, but I'll make out."

"You going to tell Miss Jean?"

I looked him in the eye. "Are *you?*"

"I guess not. But you have your dad come to me if he needs help, OK?"

"Sure, Coach." I knew I would never do it. "Were you at the picnic?"

"Yes, I was."

"And was Debra there, too?"

He gave me a smile. "Yes, she was. Why?"

"Oh, no reason."

He thought about that, then shrugged and said, "Let's go get a pizza, Barney."

I went with him, and he did his best to make me

feel better, but I would hate for anyone to know what I did after I got home that night. That is, after I told Jake and Joe the bad news about the watermelons. I went for a long walk with Tim. Going on thirteen wasn't old enough to keep me from acting like a little kid sometimes. That night, oldest or not, I buried my face in Tim's sleek side and cried. And I promised myself that if we were ever moved off this spot in Goober Holler, it would only be after I'd done everything I could to stop it!

Then I wiped my face on my sleeve and went back to the house to get some sleep.

11
Good-bye, Aunt Ellen

DURING July and August Clyde came five times to visit us, showing himself around town to keep people fooled. Before summer was over, we'd managed to sell about fifty watermelons, mostly because Coach Littlejohn bought them for church gatherings. He'd take a load and break them open beforehand. That way he could throw the bad ones out and pay for the good ones. We made close to one hundred and fifty dollars, and we kept that in a special fund with the two hundred dollars Jake had made from the chicken bet.

Now that the first of January was only five months away, I thought about that note all the time. We tried to save some out of the money that came from Chicago every month, but it took all of that for us just to live.

I was still going out with Tim alone a lot, but sometimes I went with other hunters, too. Once when Uncle Dave and I were walking back from a hunt near Caney, he began telling me about the money that professional coon hunters make.

"Why some fellers have made a fortune in coon dogs, Barney. The dog that won the National two years ago earned over $150,000 for his owner in just one year. 'Course that was in stud fees."

"Gee, that's a lot of money."

"Sure is. 'Course some fellers around here do pretty well on hides."

"On hides?"

"There's a fur season from December first to the last day of January. Man can kill all the raccoons he wants and then sell the hides."

"How much does a fella get for a hide?"

"Right now about twenty dollars."

I did some quick multiplying in my head. "Why, you might make a lot of money hunting coon."

"Well, it ain't all a piece of coconut pie, Barney. Lots of work, lots of luck in it. Most fellers who make the money run traps and dogs both. Even then you gotta know coons and you need good luck."

I didn't say anything to Uncle Dave, but from that day

I began trying to get ready for the fur season. January first was coming awful fast, and we would either have to have a thousand dollars to hand over to Simmons—or we would have to give up our home.

School started, and it wasn't bad this time. I had algebra—which I hated—but at least I knew a few people. Debra was in most of the classes I had, and so was Tony Randell. He kept asking me to come out for the basketball team, and I kept telling him I didn't have time.

I did pretty well as far as grades were concerned, and so did Jake and Joe. People in Cedarville were getting used to the Bucks and all the crazy things we'd done. Clyde made his fatherly appearances, and "Mom" was usually in Kentucky visiting her folks. The school tried to get "Mr. and Mrs. Buck" in PTA once or twice but left us alone after nothin' but rejection. The First Baptist Church didn't last much longer in their efforts to recruit us.

Uncle Dave never said a word, but he knew something wasn't right. He had too much sense not to know that a man and a wife have to be on a place more than he saw our "Ma" and "Pa." What I came to believe was that Uncle Dave—and maybe Debra—thought my parents were split up and had just dumped us to take care of ourselves.

But that was OK. I figured everything was going as

well as it could. Until I got those letters from Miss Jean. Then I started getting flat out scared.

> I know you boys are enjoying your visit, but the judge isn't quite satisfied with the reports on your aunt and uncle. I haven't been completely sure myself that Mr. and Mrs. Buck will be acceptable as permanent guardians. When I come in November for an official visit, perhaps I can look into the matter more fully.

"Good night!" Jake said when he read that. "If she ever looks into Uncle Roy and Aunt Ellen, we're sunk!"

"We can't stop her from coming, though." I stared at Jake. "Why can't you think of something? You're the one with the head full of schemes."

He glared at me and then stalked off without a word. For the next few days he was thinking, which was usually bad news. This time, I was hoping he could come up with something that would save us.

One Sunday morning in October, on our way to the highway where Coach picked us up, Jake came up with his great scheme. "We gotta finish Aunt Ellen off!"

I just stared at him.

"Yep," he said, nodding his head firmly. "It's gotta be done, Barney."

"I don't see—"

"Look, we got no chance at all of fooling Miss Jean like we did before. The first time she sees you in daylight, disguise or no disguise, she'll know it's you. So there's only one answer: Aunt Ellen has to have a nice funeral."

"Kill off our aunt?" I asked. "It sounds . . . immoral. Not to mention impossible."

"No such thing," Jake said, erasing Aunt Ellen with one wave of his hand. "We can work it out."

I thought about that until we got home from church. While we fixed dinner, I brought it up again. "I believe you're right, Jake. But I don't see how we're gonna do it. We can't have a funeral—that takes money. Besides, you have to have a death certificate and all kinds of stuff."

"Sure, if it happens *here!"* He grinned.

"Where else would it happen?"

"In Kentucky, of course." Jake had thought it all out, and I knew I was desperate 'cause the more he talked, the more possible it sounded. "Look, for going on a year we've been telling about how sick she is and how she's always visiting in Kentucky. All we have to do is just *say* that she died."

"We'd go to the funeral, wouldn't we?" Joe asked. He'd been listening carefully. "Like we did when Mom and Dad died?"

That was the first time any of us had mentioned Mom

and Dad. I looked at him, but he had said it so naturally that I knew he was over the worst of the pain.

"Sure we would. We would have to be gone three or four days to make it good."

"So we just go somewhere for three days." Jake shrugged and finished heating some beans. Then he dumped them into a bowl, which he placed on the table. "We send a note to Mr. Jenkins to cover our absence. Then we come back and that's it."

"We have to tell Miss Jean and the judge," I argued. "It might be less likely for them to let us stay with a single man instead of a couple."

"Nothing would be less likely than letting us stay with you as Aunt Ellen," Jake said firmly. "I really think it's our only chance, Barney."

The more I thought about it, the more I agreed with the idea. We had only three weeks, because Miss Jean was coming the first of November. The next day I told Jake and Joe what we were going to do.

"We can't afford to go stay in a motel. What we'll do is camp out in the woods for three days. Then if somebody comes to the house, they won't catch us."

"What?" Jake shouted, then shook his head. "I'm not gonna live under a tree for three days. It'll probably rain."

"You won't be outside," I said, trying to calm him down. "We'll stay in Bandit Cave."

"Bandit Cave! What's that?" Joe asked, his eyes suddenly bright. "It sounds exciting."

"Uncle Dave told me about it. He said he used to go there with Grandpa when they were young. He said it's about five miles from here, right through the back of our place and through the ridges that you can see sticking up over that way. Grandpa and Uncle Dave used to camp there when they were hunting. We'll take enough food and blankets to survive."

"We'll get snakebit," Jake said matter-of-factly.

"There are no snakes out in October!" I told him.

"Then we'll get attacked by wolves, or something like that," Jake said. "I don't like it."

Jake may not have liked it, but we were going to do it. I wrote the school a note and gave it to the bus driver the next day. It was from our "uncle," explaining that his wife, Ellen, had died and that we were going to Kentucky for the funeral. We would be back later in the week.

We packed up some camping stuff and a lot of groceries—all we could carry in bedrolls, the way Uncle Dave had shown me. Then around ten o'clock, right after breakfast, we locked the door and headed out.

Tim led the way. We crossed our land and soon we were going through Mr. Simmons' timber. Uncle Dave had taught me a lot, so I pointed out birds and different trees to my brothers. "That's a pileated woodpecker—

biggest woodpecker there is. Only lives in dead trees." Later on I pointed out a boar coon stuffed to his eyebrows with wild grapes. Tim found the critter, and I knew what it was by the sound Tim made.

We stopped often to rest and snack. Joe's legs weren't used to all the walking, and neither were Jake's. I didn't want them to get so tired that it wasn't fun anymore. While they rested, I studied the map Uncle Dave had given me awhile back. He'd marked the spots where the coons were thickest—and that included Bandit Cave. I'd figured it would be fairly easy to find, and sure enough it was.

About twelve noon we got to a long ridge that ran north and south. According to the map, a big stream cut east almost in the middle of it, and Bandit Cave was about two miles down that stream in a big cliff made of limestone.

We found the stream first, a pretty one that seemed to be alive with fish. I led Jake and Joe upstream, keeping on the east side, and told them to look for a big tall rock that looked like a bear head. That was what Uncle Dave had said to look for. "Timber mighta grown up in all these years, but I bet that rock's still there."

"There it is!" Joe saw it first. Soon we were standing inside a cave about as large as a good-sized barn. It was cut back about thirty feet, and the ceiling was maybe twenty feet high. We made our beds in a little niche at one end where the rock hung over, then put our food on a five-foot ledge to keep it safe from varmints.

We were all excited, and since there was still plenty of daylight left, we went exploring. I found a spring not too far from the cave with the coldest water I'd ever tasted. Then Joe got the thrill of a lifetime when he looked down at the ground and found an arrowhead. We felt like real pioneers, and I had to make Jake and Joe go back so we could start a fire and cook supper.

That night we lay down after eating a sinful amount of hamburger and potato chips. It was quiet in the cave. We could hear the coyotes starting to bark and carry on, but it sounded far away. The fire snapped and popped as a burning limb fell, but it was really peaceful.

"This is all right!" Jake sighed. He looked at his half-eaten Mounds bar and wrapped it up. "You think we could go fish in that creek tomorrow?"

"We can do anything we're big enough to do," I said sleepily.

"Boy! What a way to live," he said with another sigh.

We lay there for some time until we decided to go out and look at the stars. "Boy, there must be a million of those stars!" Jake said.

"There's more than that," Joe said and started telling us what he had learned in science. While he was talking, I heard something. I couldn't quite make it out, but it seemed to be coming from a long way over to my left.

Finally I said, "Do you guys hear anything?"

They both listened. "I can hear *something.* What is it?" Jake asked.

"Sounds kind of hollow. Like at the bottom of a well," Joe said.

"Maybe wolves or coyotes," Jake said, then the sound faded away.

We listened for a long time. Whatever it was, it was gone, so we finally went to sleep.

The next two days were about the closest thing to heaven we'd ever stumbled across. The creek was so full of fish we had to get behind a tree to bait our hooks—those fish nearly jumped out of the water the minute we pulled a worm out! We caught a mess of juicy rock bass, plump and full of fight! The woods were full of muscadines, too, and clusters of late wild grapes, sweet as honey. We ate grilled fish and fruit until we were almost ready to pop.

During the day, we played games like little kids—tag and crazy blindman's buff. We ran coons the first two nights; the countryside was packed with them. But each night we would hear that same weird, muffled sound. Finally on the third day I said, "I'm gonna go over and find out what that racket is."

Of course, Jake and Joe had to go, too. We waited until nearly dark, then went in the direction the sound seemed to come from. I'd allowed just enough time to get there with just a bit of light left, so we crossed the creek and went through a big stand of pines. From time to time, as we got closer, we heard that same muffled sound. None of us could figure it out.

Eventually the sound got louder. I motioned for Jake and Joe to start crawling. We went across a little clearing on our hands and knees, Tim creeping along right beside us, and then we inched through some briars that cut our skin. Finally I held up my hand and whispered, "I think it's over there."

I crawled alone for about a hundred feet, cutting my hands on the sharp rocks and wearing the knees of my pants to shreds. Coming to a thick hedge of briars, I stood up to look over, but I couldn't see much except for a building directly in front of me. It looked like an old barn. The strange noise was coming from inside it.

That was all I had time for, because I heard somebody saying something. Out of the corner of my eye, I saw a dark form come between me and the sky, cutting off what light there was. Then the person said, "Who's there?"

I could have stopped to talk, but it didn't seem like the right time for it. I whirled around and sprinted across the rocky floor as fast as I could.

Two gunshots rang out. It sounded like a twelve gauge splitting the night, and something stung the tip of my right ear! I kept running, but not straight toward Jake and Joe. I cut to my right and poured on the steam.

Blam!

One more shot. Then I was into the tree line. I cut around behind where my brothers were. When I got close I said, "Let's *go!*"

They had been waiting—Jake had his hand over Tim's muzzle, keeping him from barking—and we all took off. We ran hard until we were gasping for breath. I didn't hear anybody coming after us, so we all stopped. Jake leaned up against a tree. "Who was *that?*" he wheezed.

"Guy with a shotgun," I said.

"Was he shooting at *us?*" Joe asked.

I touched my ear and looked at my finger. Without a word I held it out, and they could see the bright drop of blood in the fading light. "He tried to kill me," I said, not quite believing it myself. "Let's get out of here!"

It took us longer to get back to the cave since it had gotten dark. I was glad to have the moonlight to guide us. It was too risky to use my flashlight.

When we got to Bandit Cave, we were exhausted. Jake and Joe fell asleep pretty fast, but I lay awake a long time. The next morning we had breakfast—dry cereal and some apples—and packed our stuff. It was too dangerous for us to stay at the cave any longer, especially if we wanted to build a fire.

We hurried back to Goober Holler. No nature appreciation this time. Our minds were on the close call we'd had the night before. "Who do you think that was, Barney?" Joe asked.

I'd just about made up my mind. "Well, it was probably moonshiners. Uncle Dave says a lot of them are still around here. And he said to stay just as far from them as you can get! He said they'll shoot at the drop of a hat."

"Well, I don't have plans for going back there!" Jake said. "Not Joe and me."

"Me neither," I added.

When we got to our house, we took our time unpacking and spent most of the time just relaxing. We went to school the next day, and everybody we knew acted awkward. People wanted to say something nice and comforting, but you could tell they were having trouble finding the right thing to say.

"I feel like a danged hypocrite!" I whispered to Jake. "Trying to act sad over somebody who never existed."

"Just hush up and enjoy it," Jake said. "There are worse things than having people be nice to you. The next thing you know it might be the other way around."

I just wasn't a philosopher like Jake. When Debra stopped me by the water fountain and looked up at me with sad eyes, I almost said, "For crying out loud, Debra, nobody died!" But I didn't. Actually, I *liked* getting a little sympathy. When she said, "I'm so sorry about your mother," I tried to look teary-eyed and pitiful.

"Comes to all of us, I guess," I said.

"You're being so brave about it, Barney! I think you're just wonderful."

I was no better than Jake. I just soaked up the sympathy.

Rotten. That was what I was. Just plain *rotten!*

12
The Great Fish-Out

THREE weeks after the "funeral," Miss Jean came for her visit.

When she and Coach Littlejohn came driving in together, nobody was surprised. We knew they had been writing each other. Besides, Coach had worked his way through the pretty girls of Clark County alphabetically, but when Miss Jean had shown up he'd quit right in the middle of the *M*s.

"Barney! I believe you've grown another inch!" Miss Jean squealed, then reached up a little to give me a hug. She did the same to Jake and Joe.

"You look good, Miss Jean," I said.

"Not bad—for a city girl," Coach said, smiling at her.

She was wearing a snow-white suit with a real pretty blouse. I'd say that she looked a lot better than anything you see at the sale barn on Saturday.

We went into the house, and she didn't even mention Aunt Ellen or ask for Uncle Roy. I breathed a sigh of relief.

"Get your go-to-meeting clothes on." Coach grinned. "We're all going out to eat—a celebration." He was duded up, too. He always looked as if he had just stepped out of a fashion magazine, but I'd never seen this outfit before: a cream dress shirt with his initials on the collar, a tweed blazer with those patches on the elbows to make it look sophisticated, and a pair of dark dress jeans.

"Boy!" Jake said, staring at him. "If you drop dead, we won't have to do a thing to you!"

The three of us scurried around and got on our good clothes, but when we were ready to leave, Joe said, "Wait just a minute. I've got something for Miss Jean." He rushed off to the room he used for his inventions and came back lugging a box so heavy he nearly dropped it. I caught it and set it on the table.

"What is it this time, Joe?" Coach asked. "A perpetual motion machine?"

"Nope, it's a mixer."

"You mean a food mixer?" I asked.

"This is no store-bought mixer." Joe sniffed at the

idea. "I made it myself." He pulled a heavy oak frame from the box and put the carton on the floor. "This is for you, Miss Jean. You've been so good to us, I wanted to do something for you."

I felt like a jerk! Why hadn't I thought of doing something like that?

"What a nice thought, Joe!" Miss Jean gave him a kiss, then asked, "How does it work?"

"Well, it's got only one beater, 'cause I couldn't think of any way to make two mesh up. But I think one ought to be enough. See, you put the bowl here and the top swings back. And then you put the beater in here. . . ." He fastened the beater in the jaws he had made for it. "And then you're ready."

"What's in the top?" Coach asked.

"Oh, that's the motor. It's a little heavy, so I put these springs to balance it. See how easy it works?"

Miss Jean swung the head back and forth. "Why, that *is* easy. Here, you try it, Dale."

We all admired it and bragged about how nice it was, and I was real proud of Joe. Finally he said, "I've never actually used it with batter and all. Let's try it now."

"It's pretty late," Coach said, looking at his watch.

"It won't take but just a minute." Joe was so eager to show how it worked that Miss Jean agreed. The first thing I knew I was getting out the stuff to make a chocolate cake. Miss Jean measured out the flour, butter, and other ingredients into a big bowl, and Joe took over.

"All of you get in close," he said. "This switch turns it on. Watch now."

We all got in as close as we could. Just as Joe threw the switch and the thing started humming, I had a funny feeling that something was wrong. But it was too late to pray then!

The little motor revved up, and Joe lowered the beater with one flip of his wrist into the batter.

There was a sudden slapping sound, and in a split second the bowl was empty! I knew what was wrong then! It was like a bomb had gone off, blowing that chocolate batter into a million splatters!

I got a big chunk right in the eye. Coach must have been caught with his mouth open, because he got a ton right down his throat. He was reeling and gagging, trying to get it out. Jake was bellowing and falling around all over the place. Then I got my eye cleared out and saw the mess!

The whole kitchen was a polka-dotted mess! Flecks and gobs of chocolate mix had splattered the walls and the ceiling, which we had just painted a nice yellow. Miss Jean was standing there with brown globs all over her face and suit. She was opening and closing her mouth like a thirsty bird. I don't think she could make up her mind whether to laugh or cry. Neither could I.

Tim had come in and was running around licking the walls. That dog sure liked sweets!

Jake looked like a short, fat leopard. He started for Joe with fire in his eyes, and I had to grab him before he could get to Joe.

Then I noticed that the only one who didn't have any mix on him was Joe! He'd been standing behind that fool invention, so the rest of us got all the blessing.

Coach finally spit out the last of his batter. "Joe, what kind of motor did you use?"

Joe swallowed hard and looked around at the mess. Finally he said in a weak voice, "It was an old washing machine motor."

Coach started laughing so hard he had to sit down. "Those things run over three thousand revolutions per minute!" he shouted, and that set him off again. At that point, we all had to join in. It was laugh or cry, and we all laughed until we hurt. We would get settled down and then someone would say something like: "Look how nice and neat the spots are on the ceiling!" And off we'd go again.

Finally I said, looking around at all of us, "No eating out for us."

"No, they'd throw us all out." Coach laughed.

"I tell you what," I said. "Let's fix us a real meal here. We're as good as that restaurant any old day!"

So, that was what we did. We made hush puppies and

cooked some of the tender young bass I had pulled out of the pond that day. We had potatoes, cornbread, onions, and a lot of other stuff. It took us a long time to eat and clean up, but we had fun. Then we played Monopoly, and Miss Jean finally won the game at two o'clock in the morning.

"I *must* go!" she said after staring at her watch as if it was lying to her. "I've never had such a good time. Makes me realize what I'm missing—not having a family, I mean."

"Never too late to begin," Coach said, his eyes innocently fixed on the spotted ceiling.

She got all red, and they left saying they'd see us the next day.

"Maybe we can keep her entertained so much she'll forget to look too closely at us," I said as we were gathering up the play money and stuff from the game.

Jake slapped the lid on the box and gave me a wise grin. "I sort of think Coach Littlejohn will take care of that!"

He was right. The next day Miss Jean began to get serious about us—what to do about "Dad" and all that. Then Coach Littlejohn would say, "What about catching that movie in Malvery?" and off they would go. She'd fuss at him for taking up all her time, but she'd be putting her hat on when she was doing it.

The upshot was that she stayed a week at the Holiday

Inn near Cedarville, but she didn't have that much time to pay attention to the Bucks of Goober Holler. We were safe.

For a while, at least.

Toward the middle of November, we were still way shy of the money it would take to pay the note. We talked about it a lot, and I hoped something would come up, but I didn't know what it would be.

I went with Coach to Little Rock on Thursday to attend a special conference. He said I needed a little change and he needed company, so I went. We had a great time in Little Rock. As far as I could tell, he didn't go to all the meetings I thought he was supposed to, but we did a lot of fun things! We played miniature golf and went swimming at the Y. We saw two movies and ate out for every meal. It was so much fun that I was almost able to forget that dad-burned note!

We got home around nine o'clock Saturday morning, and when we drove up to the house, I nearly fell out of the car! The whole yard was covered with all kinds of vehicles—trucks, cars, Jeeps, and motorbikes.

"Somebody must be hurt!" I said, scrambling out of the car. Coach and I started for the house, but so many people were milling around that we had to push our way through. I was really scared, but all of a sudden Coach caught me by the arm and said, "Wait a minute."

He pointed up, and when I looked where he was pointing, I got angry. Right over the porch was a big sign painted in huge red letters:

Jake Buck's Great Fish-Out!
Win $1,000 in Cash

My head was spinning. I thought maybe I was going to faint for the first time in my life. I hated to do that before I killed Jake, though! "He's gone too far this time, Coach! He's gone *nuts!* No, that's not right. He's *always* been nuts!"

"I think we'd better go back to the pond," Coach said. "Everybody seems to be headed that way."

We joined the rush, and folks started talking to Coach. "Gonna win that big prize, Coach?" one of his friends called out. "You'd better hurry, 'cause I figure I got this thing sewed up!"

We had trouble getting close, because everybody was crowded around a little platform. On it stood the inventor of the Great Fish-Out: my idiot brother, Jake Buck!

He was as cool as you please, but he always was when he was putting it to somebody. This time he had the largest crowd of his career. I should have been proud! He was standing up and talking to them all.

"Folks, I'm going to state the rules for you. You have

them on your program, but let's keep it simple." It all seemed so strange. There was this kid talking to grown men, and they were listening as if he were Abraham Lincoln at Gettysburg. Some people just have that gift. He waved his hand around and went on.

"As you can see, ten fish will be released. Five of them will be worth ten dollars to the one who catches them." He paused. "They will have green tags. Two will wear red tags and be worth twenty dollars apiece. Two will wear blue tags and be worth fifty dollars to the one who catches them." Then he paused until there was absolute silence. "One fish," he began slowly, "will wear a white tag. He will be worth one thousand dollars!"

The crowd cheered. Several people whistled real loud. "He's crazy!" I whispered to Coach. "I mean, he's really gone over the edge this time. Coach, you gotta stop it!"

Coach looked around and said, "I don't think we can. It's already gone too far."

Jake went on with his rules. "The time limit is eight hours. No restrictions on bait or equipment. Use a feather pillow if you want to." Then he turned to a tall red-faced man wearing a state patrol uniform. "This is Sergeant Potter, who will be the official judge. Are there any questions?"

"Are you gonna check the tags on them fish, Ray?" someone yelled out.

"Better than that." The trooper grinned. "I'm going to put the tags on myself."

There was a murmur of approval, and someone said, "Let's get at it!"

"You'll have to stand back while we put the fish in," Sergeant Potter said. The crowd backed up. When he bent over a steel tank to the edge of the water, he said, "The State Game and Fish Commission furnished these fish. They're all right. Bass, about a pound a piece. Easiest kind to catch, I guess."

He picked a nice little bass out with a small net, took a pair of pliers, and fastened a green tag to the critter's fin. "There she is—worth ten bucks." He handed the fish to Jake. "The operator of this show asked that he be allowed to put the fish in at different spots, which I thought was fair."

Jake carried the fish with both hands to a spot not ten feet away. Bending over, he seemed to stroke the fish, then he said something to it. He dropped it carefully in the water, straightened up, and went back for the next fish. One by one the trooper tagged the fish, and Jake put them in.

When the trooper held up the last fish to show the white tag, a cheer went up. Jake took the fish and walked sixty yards around the pond to where a little willow bent over the water. He got down as close to the water as he could but seemed to be having trouble releasing the fish.

"Put it in!" the crowd yelled. Finally, after fumbling and almost falling in, Jake carefully lowered it beside the tree and straightened up.

He came back and said, "Now you can purchase your permit, which must be worn on your shirt at all times. Entrance fee is five dollars for adults and two dollars for kids."

He had a table set up, and we watched in amazement as he took in money hand over fist. Joe was handing out the permits as fast as he could. I felt as though I was on the *Titanic*—or maybe assigned to Little Big Horn with Custer just before the massacre.

"We'll have to get out of town, Coach," I said as we sat and watched. "They'll lynch us!"

"We'll see," Coach said. "Somehow I don't think I'm going to invest in a permit. I have too much respect for Jake's talent as a con artist."

Everyone else, though, had bought a permit and was waiting for Jake's cue to start. Finally Jake got up with money stuffed in all his pockets and said, "Go!" There was a stampede to the pond. Some of the kids almost got trampled, and soon the banks were lined with fishermen elbow to elbow. It was a good-sized pond, around two or three acres, but there wasn't much room left on the banks.

I walked over to Jake, who was counting the money, and said, "Well, brother, see you finally found a way to get us all into the state pen."

He looked up and grinned, but didn't stop counting. "Two hundred twenty, two hundred thirty . . ."

I knew he was loony, so I just went off and waited for the roof to fall in. Coach stayed close to me. When somebody called out in ten minutes, "I got one, I got one!" I nearly turned green.

A boy about ten years old came running up waving a fish in his hand, and the crowd surged around him. He came up to Jake and said, "It's got a blue tag! That's fifty dollars!"

Jake gave it a look and fished some bills out of his pocket. He patted the boy on the arm and gave him the money. "Congratulations."

"Can I try again, Jake?" the boy asked wildly, waving the fish and the money around.

"Nothing against the rules in that, is there, Sergeant?" Jake asked. When the trooper shook his head no, Jake said, "Go get another one."

Well, that set the crowd off. They milled around, changed positions, changed baits, and some of them lost control of their tongues. In fact, the trooper had to break up six fights that morning.

A green-tagged fish was caught at ten, and one of the red ones about ten-thirty. Jake didn't seem too affected by it all. He just smiled and handed out the cash as casually as if it were play money. Two greens were caught within five feet of each other in just ten minutes, so everybody came crowding and pushing to get as close as they could. A big fat man named Pat Talley from Des Arc fell in and had to be fished out—which he almost wasn't because nobody wanted to quit fishing to help him.

Not many folks had brought water, but Jake and Joe came out with coffee and Cokes at eleven o'clock. "How much for the coffee?" a man asked.

"Only one dollar a cup," Jake said matter-of-factly. When the man said it was too high, Jake added, "But it includes the sugar." They sold about forty cups of coffee and Cokes. Then at lunch, they went around with sandwiches and candy in a red wagon they'd borrowed from somewhere. All sandwiches were "only" two dollars, and I thought for sure the crowd would turn against Jake. But they didn't. They paid up, and Jake had to periodically empty his pockets into a cash box to make room for the money.

The afternoon dragged by. I thought every time somebody spoke, it meant he had that thousand-dollar fish, but no one did. By five-thirty it was dark, and a few people had gone home. Finally the trooper called out, "Time's up!" Everyone hollered and groaned, but they all got their stuff, piled into their vehicles, and left.

I looked around. The place was a mess. Papers and trash were all over the yard. It would take a day's work to clean it up. Coach and I went into the house, where

Jake and Joe were counting the money on the table. What a sight!

"How much did you pay out for the prize fish?" Coach asked.

Joe answered. "Two greens, that's twenty dollars. Two reds, that's forty dollars. One blue, that's fifty dollars. Makes one hundred and ten dollars in all."

Jake finished counting the money. "Three hundred thirty-six dollars. We spent around forty-five bucks for the drinks and sandwiches."

"I wonder what would have happened if that fish with the white tag had been caught?" I said looking straight at him.

He collected the money without blinking an eye and handed it to me. "Better put that in the bank tomorrow. There are plenty of folks in this world who aren't totally above taking what's not theirs."

As it turned out, the Great Fish-Out ended up making us Bucks look bad. Everyone said it was crooked. No one could prove anything, but it was just those "crooked Bucks" from Goober Holler up to "another trick."

One good thing was that it ran our bank account up. We had nearly six hundred dollars, but the note was due in less than two months.

A couple of days later I was scooping up pond water for the kids at school to use in a science experiment.

Suddenly my bucket hit something big. When I leaned over and reached into the water, I felt wire mesh and something move. I ran to get my net and dipped it into the water. Suddenly I felt a jerking motion and knew I'd caught a big fish. It was a bass with a white tag on its dorsal fin. I stared at it for a minute, then brought it inside the house.

"Look at this, Jake," I said.

He was doing his homework, but when he saw the fish, his jaw sagged. "Well, I'll be dipped! There's that thousand-dollar fish."

"None other," I said. "Say, look at his mouth!"

Jake came and leaned over. He peered at the fish, then looked me right in the eye. "Looks like he got caught in a wire fence of some kind."

I stared at him. "Looks to *me* like his jaws are stapled together with some kind of ring—sort of like one of those hog rings you snap on with pliers."

"It *does* look like that," Jake said, peering at the fish again. "But then there's barbed wire fence running under the water on the south end—and there aren't any hog rings, are there? Right, Barney?"

He pulled the fish out of my hands and started moving toward the porch.

"Where are you going with that fish?"

He stopped and stared at me. "Gonna clean him and eat him for supper. What else?" He gave me a pitying look. "Barney, you gotta grow up. We can't afford to waste food."

Jake and Joe ate him that night.

I would have felt like a cannibal!

The next week was Thanksgiving, and we were expecting Clyde to come for a visit. He surprised us the day before Thanksgiving with a carload of groceries and some nice warm winter jackets. What's more, one of his lady friends had knitted caps, scarves, and mittens to match our jackets.

Clyde helped us prepare stuffed turkey, two kinds of potatoes, green beans, and homemade cranberry sauce. We had three pies—pumpkin, apple, and pecan—which he picked up from a local baker. Finally, everything was ready to eat. It smelled and looked so good!

When Clyde was saying the blessing, I opened my eyes and noticed Joe had a tear running down his cheek. Jake was wiping his nose, and I wasn't feeling too happy either. Memories of other Thanksgivings—Thanksgivings with Mom and Dad—ran through my head, and I thought again about all we'd been doin' and sayin' . . . things we never shoulda been doin' and sayin'. . . .

But we did have a lot to be thankful for. We still had our house—at least for a few more months anyway—and we had some good friends like Clyde and Coach and Miss Jean. Most of all, we Buck brothers were still together.

13
Dog Thief

WHEN the first of December finally came, I knew our only hope of paying off the note was to make money from coon hides. I invested thirty-five dollars in a rusty old set of traps and got Uncle Dave to show me how to use them. I would have to run them every day after school, and that meant walking nearly five miles through rough country—but I knew I didn't have any other choice.

Every night I went out with Tim, not just to find coons, but to shoot and clean them, then haul the hides back in. In two weeks I was a zombie. I was sleeping about three hours a night—which meant I was falling asleep in class. Uncle Dave went with me several nights, but his rheumatism got so bad he just couldn't help any longer. I wouldn't let Jake or Joe go. It was just too rough. Besides, I was the oldest.

Maybe I could have made it if nothing had come up. I was averaging about one coon hide a day in the woods with Tim but getting no possums in the traps. I just didn't know enough to make it all work. All I did know was if I got one hide every day all through December, that would bring in six hundred dollars.

Just enough—if nothing happened.

The week before school was out for Christmas, we had a big intramural basketball game. I was still just playing during the day. The best players went to other schools and practiced just like the high school team.

I couldn't believe how uptight these people got over a game! They had cheerleaders and pep rallies and everything, all just for the teams in elementary and junior high.

I played in the games a little but never really got into it. The last game was between Tony Randell's team and Bubba Simmons and his group. It was on the last day of school before vacation, and just about the whole town came out to watch. The gym was packed.

I didn't really expect to play. For the first half I just sat and watched. Did the same for most of the second half. Tony's team was trailing by ten points, and I wanted to see them win, but they were having trouble hitting their shots. Finally with ten minutes left, Tony called time out. He came to the bench, and I got up with the others to listen to him.

He had a tight look on his face when he said, "We can't win this game if we can't get points! Seems like we can't get anything. . . ." He stopped then and looked right at me. Then he came over and grabbed me by the arm. "Barney, you've got to go in!"

"But, Tony, I'm no good! Can't play defense at all!"

"You can get us some points! The rest of us will have to take up the slack on defense. We can do it! Can't we, guys?" They gave a little cheer, but I could see they didn't have any more confidence in me than *I* had!

Tony didn't give me any time to argue. I found myself out there, and it was our ball. Tony ran down the court, and I just barely had time to get into position when he practically handed the ball to me. Bubba was guarding me, a big sneer on his red face. He charged into me as if we were playing football. I missed the shot, but Bubba drew a foul. And I made the two free throws.

The opposition got the ball, and I didn't even get to their end of the court. They tried a quick jump shot and missed. Our forward came up with the rebound and tossed the ball to Tony, who brought it down the court, weaving in and out. Again he just put it into my hands. All I had to do was go up and send it right in the basket. Which I did.

Now we were only six points behind. The crowd really came alive.

We went right down to the wire. Bubba found out pretty quick that we had a four-man defense, and his team made most of their shots. But we kept coming back because they couldn't stop my jump shots. Bubba tried and he drew two more fouls—which made four for him—and the score was tied with only two minutes left to play.

Bubba's side had the ball and went into a stall, hoping to get that last shot in while leaving us no time to get the ball back to our end of the court. Tony ran by me and said, "Barney, get to the other end of the court!" I ran down there feeling like a fool standing all by myself with the other guys fighting it out.

With ten seconds left, Bubba tried a lay-up that rimmed the basket, then fell outside. Tony got the rebound with only a few seconds left. He hollered, "Here it comes, Barney!" and just heaved it at me. I was lousy at catching passes from five feet away, and this one was coming from the other end of the court!

That ball came at me like a bullet, but it dropped right into my hands. I said the quickest prayer of my life just as the ball hit my palms. Somehow I grabbed it, went up, and gave it a shove with one hand in the general direction of the hoop. The buzzer went off while the ball was in the air . . . and I couldn't believe my eyes when it swished through without even touching the rim.

For a split second the gym got as quiet as a cemetery. Then the place exploded. Everybody who was for Tony's team was screaming, and the guys tried to carry me off on their shoulders—only I was way too tall for them. Coach had a big grin all over his face, and Debra bubbled with excitement.

It wasn't so bad, you know?

As I was on my way to the dressing room, I passed Bubba and his dad. They both had sour looks on their faces. All they had to do was bottle those looks, and they could poison rattlesnakes!

The guys tried to get me to go down to McDonald's and celebrate, but I had to get home to my chores. Debra stayed beside me while I was walking to the bus. She said, "You're working too hard, Barney. You look awful tired. Uncle Dave told me what you're doing to make money, about the coons and all." She got a little red and said quickly, "I'm not going to kiss you again, if that's what you're worried about, but you just remember what I told you about the money."

I must've been overexcited about the game, because I turned to her, not even caring if all the kids were listening. "Debra, you're *swell!*" I shouted. "You're the best girl in the whole world!" And then I gave her a hug and a kiss that missed her mouth but hit her on the eye. She stood there like a stone as the bus pulled out with all the kids making kissing noises.

All day Saturday I hunted and got two coons with Tim and finally one in a trap. Maybe I was learning how all this worked after all. I cleaned the hides and went to bed early for a change.

I didn't hunt on Sunday. Coach had never said a word about it, but it wouldn't have seemed right. He took us to church, then invited us over to eat dinner with him. When we got home that afternoon, Jake asked, "We gonna make it, Barney?"

I knew he was keeping up with our bank account as carefully as I was, and I shook my head. "I'm doing my best. Guess it's in somebody else's hands now."

He thought about that a long time, then nodded. "I've been thinking a lot about that lately. You figure God's gonna help us out?" I looked at him in surprise. Jake never talked about God.

"I sure hope so, Jake," I said. "I just have to trust he'll take care of us like he promised to."

He looked at me curiously. "Like he promised? What do you mean?"

We had a good long talk about all kinds of stuff—God, the Bible, our folks, just everything—then we had a snack and went to bed early. As I crawled under the covers, I thought maybe Jake wouldn't end up in the pen after all.

The next morning a heavy pounding on the front door woke us all up. The alarm hadn't gone off, and no car had driven up. "Who can *that* be?" I whispered. We all scrambled out of bed, pulled on our clothes, and tiptoed down the stairs. I peered out the window by the front door. It was Sheriff Tanner, along with Mr. Simmons and Bubba. I unlocked the door and opened it.

"Barney, I got a search warrant here," the sheriff said, handing me a paper. "Is your dad here?"

"No sir, he's . . ."

"He never is, is he?" Mr. Simmons gave a short laugh and looked mean.

"What is it, Sheriff?" I asked.

"We've got to look your place over for some stolen dogs."

"What? You think I'm a dog stealer?" I took one look at Bubba and knew right then who my accusers were. "Well, you just come on in, Sheriff. You won't find a dog in here."

"I reckon not in the house. We'll take a look around outside. You'll have to come with us."

Jake and Joe walked onto the porch, and we all followed the sheriff and the Simmonses off the porch and back behind the house. Mr. Simmons started bad-mouthing me and didn't stop until the sheriff said, "Shut up, Emmett."

It was cold. We went across the old melon patch and through a strip of dried field grass. None of us said a word until we got to the back fence.

"We'll go this way," the sheriff said. He led us through the woods along where the old barbed wire fence marked the property line. We went for about a quarter mile, and I heard a dog barking. It wasn't Tim, because we'd left him tied up at the house. Bubba had a sneaky grin on his face.

"There's a dog," the sheriff said, and we moved along until we came to a little clearing, where two Treeing Walker hounds were tied to saplings.

"That's Jim!" Mr. Simmons hollered. He ran to one of the dogs, then looked around and said, "And there's Pearl!"

I just stood there, my mouth hanging open, while they untied the dogs. "But where's Midnight? He's gone!" Mr. Simmons said. He turned around and came toward me. "You know where Midnight is, you dirty dog thief!"

"I didn't—," I started to say, but that's all I got out. Suddenly Mr. Simmons let go of his dog and hit me, smack in the face, before the sheriff could stop him. I fell against a tree and slumped on the ground. In no time at all Jake and Joe pitched into Mr. Simmons!

Jake hit him about belt high and Joe got him at the ankles.

Sheriff Tanner pulled them off and said, "You boys calm down." Then he took Mr. Simmons by the arm and said in a hard voice, "Emmett, you put one more hand on this boy, and I'll lay you out cold as a wedge! Then I'll charge you with assault and battery!" He gave him a shove and said, "Now you get out of here. I'll take care of this."

"I'll remember this next election, Tanner!" Simmons shouted. "You won't be wearing that badge for long!" Then he sneered and went off cursing, Bubba trailing after him.

"Come on, boys," the sheriff said. We followed him back to the house. "Let's warm up for a spell." He pointed toward the door. When we got inside, he just stood there looking at me for a long time, not saying anything. Finally he said, "Barney, I don't want you to say anything to me, you hear? Because I'd have to repeat it in court if I was put under oath. So just don't say anything."

"Will I . . . will I have to go to jail?"

"I'll have to take you all in. Those dogs are worth a pile of money. Besides, other dogs have been taken, and the prosecuting attorney will want to question you about that. Now, all you boys go get some clothes. You got a suitcase, Barney?"

"Yes sir."

"Well, pack it up. Take enough for a few days, pajamas and all."

"Are we going to jail, too, Sheriff?" Joe asked.

Sheriff Tanner stared at him. "No, son, but I can't leave you out here alone. I'll see you get a good place to stay. Now get packed."

We packed and went outside with the sheriff. "Lock the door," he said. "Don't want anyone breakin' in before you come back."

That was a little ray of hope—he thought we might be back. Tim was whining, and I asked, "What about Tim? He'll starve or run away."

"No, he won't. Untie him and we'll put him on the backseat. I'll keep him until this is over." We walked out to the highway, where the sheriff had left his car, then put Tim on the backseat. We piled in next to him.

It was chilly, but I felt numb for other reasons. My hands were trembling and I couldn't swallow. All I could think was *We're going to lose the place!* That was worse than going to jail!

I looked at Jake and Joe, and neither of them was crying. *That's pretty good,* I thought. Those two little kids had been kicked in the teeth in just about every way, but they weren't giving up. I sort of wished Mom and Dad could have seen that. They'd have been proud.

Sheriff Tanner pulled up at a neat white house on the outskirts of town. "Jake, you and Joe come with me."

"Where are we?" Jake asked as he scrambled out.

"My place. Come on in and meet my wife. You'll get along with her. At least every other kid I ever saw did."

The sheriff didn't even look at me when he left. Maybe he thought I was too scared to run. I probably was. While he was gone, I tried to think things out, but my head was just swirling around. I tried to pray, but I wasn't too successful at that, either.

All I could get out was, "Lord . . . help!"

After a few minutes Sheriff Tanner returned and got into the car. He drove around to a big lot behind the house, where a nice dog run was. Two redbones woke up and started barking. "Put Tim in here," he said as we got out. "Have to keep him penned up, but I'll see he gets good care." Tim didn't bark or carry on when I left. He just licked my hand.

"I guess I'm ready, Sheriff." He gave me a sharp look, then we went to the jail. I felt this was a dream happening to somebody else. Or I was watching a movie and I wasn't that boy they were about to put in jail.

"Come on into my office," Sheriff Tanner said. I followed him into a small office with a desk and a few chairs. "Sit down there," he said. Then he picked up the phone and dialed a number. He talked for a few minutes with somebody, but I didn't listen too closely. Finally, he hung up.

"Barney, you're in big trouble. You need help. There's a man coming to see you, and I think he'll help you if anybody can. He's a special kind of lawyer. Lives in Pine Bluff, but he's coming over to see you first thing in the morning."

"I don't have any money for a lawyer."

"He won't ask you for any. You just talk to him. Trust him if you can. He's someone I'd want in my corner if I was in your shoes. Now you want me to get in touch with anyone else—your dad, maybe?"

He gave me one of his sharp looks, but I just said, "Coach Littlejohn."

"All right, I'll go tell him myself. He's a close friend?"

"Yes sir, and—" I broke off all of a sudden. I had been about to say Uncle Dave's name, and even Debra—but that was over for always.

He waited. "Coach is all," I said.

"All right." He got up. "Barney, I'd like to take you to my house with your brothers. It's what I do ordinarily, but this whole county is funny about dogs. They take them seriously, and if it got out that I let a prime suspect out of jail, I'd be looking for a job next election. I'll make things as nice as I can for you here."

I got up and looked him right in the eye. "You've been real good to us."

"Barney, before this thing is over it's all going to come out. I mean about your folks and everything." He stopped and put his hand on my shoulder and said quietly, "I want you to know one thing: I'm on your side."

It caught me off guard. I mean, here I'd been trying to think of some way to throw Sheriff Tanner off the track, and now he suddenly tells me that he's going to help me if he can!

"I know you boys are up to something," Sheriff Tanner said quietly, "and I don't guess I'll ever know all of it. But here's what I'm trying to say: I've got a job to do as sheriff, but I've got another job—and that's my duty as a Christian. So, you just think of me like that, if you can."

I nodded, and that sort of settled things. "I guess everybody will have to know, Sheriff."

He put me in a nice cell all by myself. He brought me a TV and a lot of books. At noon his wife brought me a meal five boys couldn't have eaten. That evening Joe and Jake came to visit. We couldn't think of much to say, so we just watched TV.

The lawyer from Pine Bluff, Henry Dempsey, came the next morning, and he was nice. We talked nearly all morning. Actually *I* talked and he listened. Then he left and I spent all day reading. It was about the same as the day before. Mrs. Tanner kept bringing me good meals that I couldn't finish, and Jake and Joe kept coming to visit and not saying much of anything.

I guess sometimes all you can do is wait.

14
Guilty!

THIS is only a preliminary hearing," Judge Pasco said. "If the court decides this morning that there are grounds for a later hearing, a date will be set. Do you understand that, Barney?"

"Yes sir." Mr. Dempsey had explained it would be that way, so I wasn't surprised. I was standing along with Mr. Dempsey in front of the judge in a small room at the courthouse. Sheriff Tanner and Coach Littlejohn were sitting next to the wall, and Mr. Helton, the prosecuting attorney, was facing us across from the table.

The judge was a tall, fine-looking man with thick, black hair and a wide mouth. He looked like someone who laughed a lot, but he was stern just then. He was friendlier looking than Judge Poindexter back in Chicago.

The one who really bothered me was Mr. Helton.

I'd been in jail for six days, and every day Mr. Helton had used up a lot of time talking to me. He was a short, squatty man with a round face, and he wore gold-rimmed glasses that kept slipping down on his nose. He had a tight little mouth, and he always shook his head after everything I said as if he couldn't believe I could be such a liar. I found out later he was under a lot of pressure from people in Cedarville to get me convicted. He sure acted like it.

"Mr. Helton, will you state the case, please?" Judge Pasco said.

Mr. Helton sort of tiptoed around a little, then said in a high-pitched voice, "Your Honor, the evidence against the defendant is so overwhelming that it won't take the court long to come to a decision."

"You don't mind if I take a little extra time, do you, Mr. Helton?"

The judge sounded so sharp that Mr. Helton got red and hurried on to say, "I beg your pardon, Your Honor. Let me just give the basic facts without comments." The judge nodded, and Mr. Helton went over the whole thing. In effect, what he said was that I had been caught red-handed with the stolen property, and there was an eyewitness to the crime. He stretched it out and did a lot of dramatic stuff.

When he finished, the judge sat for a while with his chin in his hand. Then he looked at me, and I looked at him. "Mr. Dempsey, I will allow you to speak for your client. However, I must tell you that in the face of the evidence I have decided to set a hearing. Say for January 15."

"I'll present my case at that time, Your Honor," Mr. Dempsey said. He had come over from Pine Bluff many times, and it didn't surprise me when he said that. He'd already told me what would probably happen.

"I'm going to order the sheriff to release you, Barney," the judge said. "Bail has been set and paid. You will not leave this county for any reason whatsoever without the permission of the court. Do you understand that clearly?"

"Yes sir, but who paid the bail, Judge Pasco?"

The judge's face was smooth. "I am not informed on that question. One thing more, the moment your father comes home I want to see him." He nodded, and Mr. Dempsey led the way out of the room.

Outside, Mr. Dempsey said, "I don't know who put up the bail, but I'll try to find out." Then he looked at Coach and asked, "Dale, you'll watch out for them?"

"Sure, it's Christmas vacation, so I've got plenty of free time."

"I'll be around, too," Sheriff Tanner said. "Let me know if there's anything I can do."

Mr. Dempsey gave a sour smile. He was a sort of young-old man with a wrinkled face, but he looked like an athlete, the way he moved and all. "Well, it would be nice if you could find that dog *and* whoever took him. That's our best shot."

"I'm working on it."

"Call me if you find anything. It looks pretty bleak on the surface, Barney, but don't you quit on me. Things aren't always what they appear." He gave me a warm smile, shook hands all around, and left.

Coach said, "Come on, Barney. I'll take you home."

"What about my clothes?"

"We'll go pick them up. And then we'll stop by the Tanners and get your brothers and dog."

Sheriff Tanner walked to the car with me without saying a lot. He gave my arm a punch when I got in. "Maybe you and me can go after a coon some night, huh?"

"Sure, and thanks a lot, Sheriff."

"Going to be a cold night," Coach said.

"Sure is." I wasn't much in the mood for talking.

I knew Coach was trying to cheer me up, but I felt worse than ever for some reason. I should've been happy. The sun was shining, and it was a beautiful winter day with a nippy wind and the smell of wood smoke. But I was a criminal. They'd taken my fingerprints and made pictures of me. I had a record. Oh, they had been nice, but I was a criminal. Out on bail.

"Barney," Coach said suddenly. "You can't quit. I know that's what you feel like doing. It's what *I'd* feel like doing if I were in your place. But I know it's going to be all right."

"I sure don't see how." I was so tired and low that it looked like the burnt-out end of everything to me. "I just don't see how *anything* can work out."

Coach gave me a worried look. "I guess that's what real faith is—believing when there's nothing to believe *in.* If we could *see* something, it wouldn't be faith, would it?"

"N-no, I guess not."

"Maybe I haven't been fair with you."

"Fair? What do you mean? You've been real good to me. Why, you've been the best friend I've had in this whole town."

"No, I don't think so," Coach said thoughtfully. "I've beat around the bush and tried to say what I felt as honestly as I could—but I've never come right out with what I've really wanted to say."

I just sat there, and he seemed to be waiting. Finally I said, "Coach, you can say anything you like to me."

He gave me a quick glance, then said, "All right, I will. The thing I feel you need most, Barney, is to let

Jesus Christ come into your life. But I know you've heard that before. You've been in church most of your life, but there's more to it than that."

"What do you mean, Coach?"

He shifted in his seat, then seemed to settle something in his mind. "Barney, you must have heard about the new birth, about being 'born again.' That's what happened to me a year ago. I'd been a church member for a long time, but it had been a meaningless thing. I'd tried to be a 'good Christian' most of my life, but it was no good. Everything in my life just seemed to be falling apart. Life was the *pits!* And then, something happened to me." He suddenly stopped.

"Well, what was it?" I asked.

He looked at me. "I found out that my life had been a fraud, Barney," he said gently. "All my efforts to *be* a Christian had been a waste. But praise the Lord, I turned to Jesus Christ. I just gave up on myself, and that's when it happened!"

"What?"

We were just pulling into the Tanners' driveway. He didn't answer until we were in front of the house. He didn't shut the engine off but turned to me and said, "I was saved, Barney! I know how corny that sounds today, but that's the Bible word for it. I just got so deep in despair that I was ready to hang it all up. And then a friend of mine gave me a little help and told me to call on Jesus Christ. And I did. Literally. I just called on Jesus and he came into my life, and since that day, why, I've been different."

He looked at me, and I could tell he was real serious about all this. "That's what I think you ought to do, Barney—call on Jesus Christ. He'll help you with this thing that's been bothering you."

I sat there trembling like a leaf. Coach was right! More than anything else in the world, I needed to have the peace that Coach seemed to have. But I was so confused! How could I call on God to save me when I'd gotten myself into this mess?

We sat there for a while, and finally I shook my head. "Coach, I don't know what to do, but I need *something!*"

He grinned at me and shook his head. "No, you need Some*body.* Now let's go get Jake and Joe and see how old Tim's doing."

They were all glad to see me. Before the rest of us got into Coach's car, Mrs. Tanner gave me a hug and told me not to worry.

When he dropped us off at the house, Coach said, "It's going to be all right, Barney. I'm praying for you, and I'll be around!" Then he drove off.

I waved at him, then turned to Jake and Joe. "Well, here I am," I said with a smile. "The Jesse James of Goober Holler. A famous outlaw, and only going on thirteen."

"Ah, come on, Barney," Joe said. "You're no outlaw."

"But I'm still the prime suspect." I told them about the hearing and how I wasn't much better off than I had been in jail. "I think Bubba put those dogs there. I don't think he had anything to do with Midnight's being gone, though. I was watching Bubba when Mr. Simmons noticed Midnight was missing. Bubba was really shocked. He's not that good an actor! He was shocked right out of his gourd."

"You think the dognapper got him?" Joe asked.

"That's what I think. It's the only thing that makes sense." I slumped down in a chair. "Well, we've got other things to worry about. For one thing, I don't see how in the world we're going to pay that note. And you know what Mr. Simmons will do then!"

"How much do we have?" Joe asked.

"We got exactly $564.24," Jake said. "And we need at least that much more. Do you think you can get enough coons to make that much, Barney?"

"At twenty dollars a hide? No way! Not with all the time I'm gonna be sitting in a courtroom . . ." My voice trailed off when I saw the looks on their faces. I could have kicked myself! I tried to work up some kind of a grin. "But you never can tell. I'm going to be caught trying!"

I guess I won't ever forget that week. It was a couple of days before Christmas. The three of us chased coons night and day. I showed Jake how to run the traps and how to skin the critters out. That way I could run Tim all night, and Joe and Jake could do the day work. My leg muscles were really strong now. It wasn't anything for me to run twelve or even fifteen miles in one night.

Once I got on the trail of a real runner. Most coons will tree, but when you get one that wants to run, he can cover a lot of country. I chased him for hours and finally nailed him in a big hollow log. I flushed him out and shot him, and for the first time looked around to see where we were. We hadn't gone a hundred feet before I realized that the creek we had to cross was the one that ran by Bandit Cave. The thought scared me at first, but I just shrugged. Couldn't be in much more trouble than I already was, you know? So why not poke around that place a little more?

OK, so it wasn't smart. I mean, I was out on bail, facing a jail sentence, and about to lose my home. And what did I do? I went looking for a man who'd tried to shoot me the only time I ever saw him! But I played it safe. I crawled in from an angle different from the one I had used before. The fir trees were thick, and I got close enough to see the old barn. This time there was no noise at all from anywhere on the place. I was just getting ready to leave when I saw something I hadn't noticed the last time—a shack over against the tree line.

A little light filtered out of the window, and I could smell wood smoke.

I didn't try to see anymore. Whoever it was and whatever he was doing—well, it just wasn't worth getting shot over! When I got home, I didn't say anything to the boys about it, but I couldn't get it out of my mind.

By Friday, which was Christmas Eve, we could all see we were out of luck. We took all the skins we had to Mr. Layton's store. After he paid us, we stood outside for a while, trying to think of something.

"What it comes to," I said, "is that we have a little less than seven hundred and fifty dollars—and that note is over twelve hundred dollars with interest."

"Can't we sell something?" Joe asked, but he knew as well as I that we had nothing to sell.

"There's only one thing to do," Jake said. "We got to go ask Mr. Simmons for more time."

I stared at him as if he had just grown another head. "Jake, you're smarter than *that!* Why, he hates me!"

"Sure, I know, but we've been hearing about miracles at church. And this *is* Christmas. Maybe he'll be like old Scrooge in that story—you know, get real generous."

"That *would* be a miracle," I snorted. Jake kept on talking, and Joe kept saying we ought to try something.

Then I got this funny feeling. Sometimes so many things go bad that you finally get the I-don't-cares. I got up and said, "Sure, why not? All he can do is put the dogs on us!"

We had a cold walk over to the Simmonses' place, and the closer we got, the wilder the idea seemed. But I was busy with another crazy thought that had come to me over and over again. Ever since we'd started lying and deceiving people—I mean *I* had—something kept telling me, *You'll pay for this!*

I kept thinking that going to see Mr. Simmons was part of the payment. I would rather have slid down a forty-foot razor blade into a vat of alcohol than go beg that man for anything. But what Uncle Dave had said kept coming back to me, "We all got to eat our peck of dirt!"

There were lights on all over the house. We could hear Bing Crosby singing "White Christmas" when we went up the steps and rang the bell. An old woman, probably a distant relative, answered the door. "You're just in time for the punch and cake," she said. "Come right this way."

I knew she thought we were friends of the kids, so we traipsed right in after her into a huge room at the end of the hallway. A huge cedar tree loaded down with lights stood against one wall, presents stacked up to the branches under it. A long table filled with a punch bowl and dishes piled with candy and cookies was along the opposite wall. The family was gathered nearby.

Debra's eyes got as big as dinner plates when she saw us. Mr. Simmons' narrowed into tiny little slivers. Bubba nearly dropped his cookie, and Mrs. Simmons gave her husband a nervous look. Uncle Dave was sitting on a straight-backed chair by a window. He got up and stared at us with an odd look in his dark eyes.

Then Mr. Simmons went off like a siren. "What are you doing in my house?" he thundered. His face got beet red and he rushed at me, but Debra and her mother grabbed his arms. He might have thrown me out the window if they hadn't.

Finally they got him calmed down long enough for me to speak.

"Mr. Simmons, I'm real sorry to bother you on Christmas Eve, but the note comes due in just a few days. We came to give you what we got—about seven hundred and fifty dollars and—" I choked before I could say the rest. "And . . . and to ask if we could have another month to get the rest of it."

He stared at me, then threw back his head and laughed, but it wasn't a good kind of laugh. Nobody else joined in, except Bubba. Finally Mr. Simmons stopped. "You got your gall, Buck. I'll give you that! Steal a man's dog, then come and beg for mercy! Well, you can just think about it when you get sent up!" He started hollering again, but Debra pulled at his arm and tried to talk to him.

"Daddy, Barney didn't—"

He jumped and shouted at her. "Keep out of this! I've heard about you followin' around after this white trash like a lovesick calf! There'll be none of that, you hear? I guess I can still find me a peach tree switch!"

Bubba was grinning with all his might. He laughed. "I don't guess you'll have to worry about him, Pa. Not where he's goin' pretty soon!"

Then Uncle Dave spoke up. "You sure this is the way you want to act, Emmett?" He was staring at his son, his eyes sharp as diamonds. He hadn't talked loudly, but Mr. Simmons jumped as if he'd been shot.

"Now, Pa, don't you start!" Mr. Simmons said. "I know how you been tryin' to make somethin' out of this kid, but you're always doing somethin' like that. And most times you get stabbed in the back from those you try to help. Now you just stay out of this, will you, please?"

"Mr. Simmons, I didn't steal your dogs," I said. "That's what I came to tell you tonight. I didn't really think you'd do anything about the note."

"You liar! Get out of my house!" Mr. Simmons stomped down the hall and held the door open wide. "Get out and stay away from my family. You hear me?"

There wasn't anything else to stay for. I took one look at Debra, who was crying, and one at Uncle Dave, who was staring at his son as if he'd never seen him before.

We turned and walked out of the house. The door slammed, and I heard a big argument start. Mr. Simmons and Bubba were yelling, and Uncle Dave was saying something in a hard, dry voice.

The walk back home just about froze us to death. We ran into the house and got ready for bed. I don't think any of us thought about Santa Claus that night. I hoped Jake and Joe weren't thinking about our *last* Christmas—when Mom and Dad had tucked us in and then had put the presents under the tree. I hoped they weren't feeling too bad about not even having a tree this year. . . .

But I thought they probably were.

15

'Twas the Night before Christmas . . .

WHY didn't the dognapper take the other two dogs?"

Jake spoke up in the darkness, and neither Joe nor I was asleep. I rolled over. By the light of the full moon, I could see Jake sitting straight up in bed. "I can't quit thinking about that."

"Yeah, me too," I said and sat up. "Doesn't make any sense. And you know what else bugs me? That barn at Bandit Cave. There's something funny about it, and I can't think what it is."

We sat there in bed thinking. Then after a long time I said, "You know what? Maybe I got something!"

"What're you thinking?" Jake asked.

"Well, you know about how all the dogs have been

disappearing? Think about this, Jake—most of the dogs have been taken from some place in the area around here. You remember two or three times, though, dogs were snatched the same night, and we wondered how the dognapper could cover so much territory. Well, I think he's got a headquarters where he keeps them all—and Bandit Cave is just about in the center of the county. It's right in the middle of the wild country where people don't go much, but there are towns and farms all around it, you know?"

"Hey! That's *right!"* he said, excitement rising in his voice. "Whoever it is could get around the whole county and be back there pretty quick!"

"Tell you something else," I went on, "you know how we thought it might be bootleggers? Well, it's not."

"How do you figure that, Barney?" Joe asked.

"I heard Uncle Dave talking to some guys who *used* to be bootleggers, and they talked about what sort of place you need. Bandit Cave just doesn't fit. Too open, mostly." Then I threw the covers back and started pulling on my clothes.

Jake and Joe piled out right away, and Jake said, "You think we can find it in the dark?"

"We can't," I answered, "because you two aren't going!"

"That's what *you* think, big brother!" Jake smiled. "Unless you tie us to the bed, we're right with you!"

"You two aren't used to foggin' around in the woods after dark the way I am," I said. "And you'd be zonked on the way."

We argued about it, and finally Jake said in his solid, stubborn way, "No sense arguing, Barney. You'd have to tie us up to leave us here. We're all going." Joe just stood beside him, nodding.

I stared at them and tried to exert some authority, but they just grinned at me while they pulled on the rest of their clothes. "All right," I grumbled, "but we have to be careful this time."

"Sure we do," Jake said with a nod. "I'd never forgive myself if I got shot by some dognapper!"

"Let's bring some hot chocolate with us," Joe piped up.

I agreed, then went to the kitchen and made some cocoa, which I poured into a quart Thermos. I also grabbed a bag of peanut butter cookies and some apples. Then I went to the living room, got the shotgun, and filled my pockets with extra shells. Jake grabbed the .22. Joe disappeared into his workroom.

"What's *that?*" I asked when he came back to the living room.

"It's a new secret weapon," Joe said, proudly holding the contraption up. "I call it the Blasting Bolo Gun. See, it's got this string with steel balls on the end, and you pull these rubber cables back—"

"We don't have time for you to explain. Just don't shoot *me* with the thing!" We went out the door and across the yard at a fast trot. Tim whined, but we didn't need him to give us away.

The moon was big and bright. *That could be a problem later on,* I thought and stopped by the side of the house.

Then it occurred to me. Here we were on a cold, dark Christmas Eve, trying to catch a thief who was probably bigger than us. Besides that, we would be going across some rugged land and hiking a good five or six miles. But the mortgage note was due on January 1, and we were a long way from paying it—and I couldn't be much help if I was locked up.

I decided we should wait until morning when it was a lot lighter out but not so dangerous, especially for my two brothers. After some coaxing, I convinced Jake and Joe we should go back home and get some sleep.

"I'll wake you in about five hours, guys. We'll have a quick breakfast, then make our little trip after the dog-napper. OK?" I said, when we hauled ourselves inside the house.

"Yeah, OK," they both mumbled and went upstairs to bed.

In the meantime, I phoned Coach, but there was no answer. *I'll just have to call him when we get back from our little adventure,* I thought. I set the alarm and dragged myself to bed.

Morning came before we knew it. The alarm went off, and we got dressed and ate quickly, gathered our stuff from the night before, and started toward the direction of Bandit Cave.

I felt better about letting us all sleep. I could tell Jake and Joe were happier to be hiking in the daylight, too.

It was Christmas Day, but no one said anything about it. I guess we were too sad to think about the last Christmas with Mom and Dad. Somehow all I could think of was their smiles when we were opening the presents.

Anyway, we walked hard for about an hour. By that time Jake and Joe were winded. They hadn't been doing as much walking as I had, and their legs were shorter. We rested for about ten minutes and talked about what we might run into when we got to the barn. I passed around the Thermos and doled out some cookies for each of us. About an hour later we were at the cave. The shack was another fifteen minutes away.

"All right, we have to decide what we want to do. He may be inside the shack," I said. "It's still early, so it's likely he'll be asleep. So here's what we'll do. We'll sneak up and surround the shack. Then, when we're all in position, I'll sing out and tell him to give himself up."

"What if he *won't?"* Jake asked. "What if he comes out shooting like last time?"

"Well, I don't know about that," I said. "Look, we're not gonna shoot anyone, Jake. If he comes out like that, just shoot up in the air and yell. Maybe he'll get scared and give up."

"Maybe I could just wing him a little?" Jake asked, waving the rifle around.

"No! Just shoot in the air—that's *all!*"

"I can get him with my Blasting Bolo!" Joe whispered.

"You'd better lay low, Joe," I said.

"Shoot! Don't treat me like a baby!"

"You do what I tell you! And you, too, Jake. Now, let's go."

We started to work our way to the barn, keeping as quiet as we could. Someone or something was inside. As we got closer, I whispered, "You hear that?"

"Yeah!" Jake breathed. "Scratching sounds. It's dogs. Right, Barney?"

"Sounds like it." We had to cross a clearing to get to the barn. I prayed that the man wouldn't come out of the shack just then.

I kept circling around, listening to the noises. Finally I crouched down and found a loose board in the side of the building. I slowly pulled it back and looked inside. It took a second for my eyes to get used to the darkness of the barn, but then I saw something.

"What do you see, Barney?" Jake kept pulling at me, and I moved over and let him take a look. He peered inside and said, "It's them, guys! It's the dogs!"

Then Joe had to look. Finally I said, "We've got him!

We've got him cold! I don't think there were any dogs here last time. Maybe he doesn't keep them long."

"There must be ten or twelve dogs inside there," Jake said. "What're we gonna do?"

"Let's get him!" I whispered. "Jake, you go over there to that big rock."

"Where're you gonna be?"

"Over there behind that big sycamore. Joe, you get over there to those bushes, you see? When I see you two are ready, I'll call the dognapper out. Be ready to holler and shoot the rifle, but only into the air!"

They disappeared like magic, and I worked my way around to the sycamore. It wasn't hard, but my heart was beating fast like an overworked watch! This wasn't like going off the catapult. The man inside had shot at us once, and he would probably try it again. There were five shells in the shotgun, but I knew I wouldn't shoot him.

In a minute Jake was leaning out over the rock, waving his rifle. I waved, and he faded back. Joe was behind the bushes, then waved his hand.

Well, it was fish or cut bait! I swallowed hard and made a wolf call as loudly as I could. "All right, you in there! Come out with your hands up!" I shouted. "We've got you covered!"

Most of the dogs made a racket and started barking at the sound. I strained my eyes trying to see the door, but nothing happened. The longer I waited, the worse it got. Finally I called out again. "We know you're in there! Come out with your hands up and you won't get hurt. Hold your fire, men!"

I hoped the man inside thought the FBI and half the police in the state were outside waiting for him. But nothing happened. *He's not in there,* I thought. In a way, I felt relieved. Now we could go back and get Sheriff Tanner, and he could take care of this.

I waited another couple of minutes. We listened, but there wasn't a sound from the shack. I was just about to call Jake and Joe, when the door of the shack broke open and a tall man bolted out of it like a shot.

Blam! Blam!

He was swinging his gun as he ran, peppering the landscape with bullets. I ducked behind a tree, hoping the others had done the same.

"Stop! Stop or I'll shoot!" I called out. Then I fired two shots in the air, and Jake started hollering. His .22 went off like a machine gun!

I jumped up and saw that the man was making his way across the open space headed toward the woods.

Blam! Blam! Blam! He kept on firing. Some bullets went through the branches over my head.

The man was getting away, and there was nothing we could do about it. The thought flashed through my mind that if he got away, we had no proof that he even existed! The prosecuting attorney could say we'd been keeping the dogs there ourselves!

I jumped from behind the tree and took off after him, hoping he had run out of shells. Jake kept shooting the .22, but it had no effect on the thief. He didn't even slow down!

He was big and fast. I knew that once he was in the woods we would lose him. I threw down the shotgun and ran as hard as I could after him, trying not to think what would happen if I caught him!

The man was right at the edge of the clearing. A good-sized drop of maybe six feet or more was near it. I had noticed it when we were there the first time. It didn't seem like much of a jump for a tall man like him. He would make it in one leap and be gone.

I gave it my best try, but he beat me to the little rise and was just about to jump when something to my right went off and made a loud noise.

Then I heard a whirring noise, and the man turned a flip! He had been about to jump down and run away, but it looked instead as if he had put his feet together, thrown his head down, and gone wheeling over that bluff!

His rifle cartwheeled off to the side and went off with a *blam!* when it hit the ground. The man did a somersault and disappeared behind the rise. I heard a heavy thud and knew he had fallen on that bed of flinty rocks. Then there was a whooshing sound like air escaping.

When I got to the edge of the bluff and peered over, he was lying on the ground. His arms were all spread out, but his feet were together.

"I got him! I *got* him!" Joe was suddenly jumping up and down on the edge of the bluff like an Indian. "I got that sucker, Barney! It was the good ol' Blasting Bolo!"

Then Jake came over, and we all scrambled down the bluff. I was afraid the man would jump up and kill us all, but he was out cold! Falling the way he had must have knocked him out.

"Quick! We gotta tie him up before he comes around!" I said. "Anybody got a piece of rope?"

"We can use the cord from the good ol' Blasting Bolo," Joe said, bending over and cutting some cords that were wound around the man's legs. "Sure hate to ruin a good bolo." Joe handed me the cords, and we rolled the guy over and tied his hands as tight as we could. I was afraid we might cut off the circulation in his hands, but Jake said that wouldn't happen.

The dogs in the barn were barking like crazy, but eventually they shut up. We stood looking at each other, all of us grinning from ear to ear. "Joe, you saved the day!" I shouted. "If he'd gotten away, we would still be in a mess."

"I *knew* the Blasting Bolo would come in handy!" he said. "Let me show you how it works." It was similar to what the cowboys in South America use, only a lot smaller. Just a ball bearing tied with cord. Joe had made the gun out of a piece of plastic plumbing pipe about two inches in diameter and had attached rubber surgical tubing to give it power. The balls shot out, and when they hit something, the cords wound around it. They had hit the dognapper around the ankles, and he had just about broken his neck from the fall.

"He's waking up," Jake said. We all watched as he rolled over and began moaning.

"What . . . what happened?" he asked. He seemed out of breath, but slowly pulled himself into a sitting position and looked around. "What do you think you're doin'? You're goin' to get in big trouble for this!"

"You might as well shut up," I said. The man was trying to stand up. "Jake and Joe, let him have it if he tries to get away." Jake smiled and pointed his gun barrel right between the guy's eyes.

I hurried to get my shotgun, hoping Jake wouldn't take me seriously. I went to the barn and checked on the dogs. And right there, tied to a post, was Midnight! I real quick untied him and held on to his rope.

"All right, bring the thief over here," I called when I stepped outside. Jake waved his rifle in the air, probably to scare the thief a little, and they all trooped over.

"Let's head to town," I said.

As we were walking, I took a good look at the thief. He was around thirty, I guessed, but he was so dirty and greasy it was hard to tell. He had long stringy hair that was partially covered by a black hat, and his eyes were wild looking. He glared at me, and I thought he looked a little nuts. He was real tall, and his arms were too long for his body. All the time he kept mumbling under his breath.

"What's your name?" I asked the man.

"I ain't tellin' you nothin'!" he snarled.

"OK by me." I shrugged. "You'll tell Sheriff Tanner, I expect."

We made our way out to a slope by the bluff and walked back toward the barn. "What about the dogs?" Jake asked.

"We'll let the sheriff take care of that," I said. "I want him to see for himself."

The dognapper didn't say a word for the next half hour as we walked. When we stopped for a breather, he started talking. "I know you—you boys live in that old house off the highway."

"That's right."

"I useta stay some in that house, till you came. I tried to fix you—with them watermelons. Thought maybe you'd clear out." He gave us a sly look and asked, "You boys been to my place before, ain't you?"

"Sure have—and you tried to kill me."

He shook his head and tried to smile, but he wasn't charming anyone. "Naw, I just tried to scare you a little bit, you see?" Then he gave us another sly glance and lowered his voice. "Look, I got money. Lotsa money. I'll pay you real good if you let me go, OK?"

I wanted him to talk, so I acted interested. "Money? You got money?"

Jake saw what was going on and said, "Aw, he doesn't have any money!"

The man's eyes bugged out, and he tried to get his hands loose. "You don't know *nothin'!*" he said. "I got lotsa dough from sellin' dogs. I got money in a jar buried back at my place."

"You're lying," I said. "Who would you sell dogs to?"

"A big place—a hospital. Out in Oklahoma City. I take whole truckloads and they buy!"

"You sell them for experiments? To a laboratory?" I asked.

He laughed hard and said, "Laboratory, sure. I sell lotsa dogs. I got a whole jar full of money!"

Now it all made sense. The stolen dogs had been of every breed—not just expensive dogs but any kind of dog you could think of had been stolen. That was why the police had been so puzzled. *Labs must not be choosy,* I guessed.

"Come on," I said. "We still have a long way to go." The man started screaming and tried to run, but we tripped him up, then shoved him in front of us.

"It's gonna be all right, isn't it, Barney?" Joe asked with a big smile.

I laughed at him and tousled his hair. "It sure is! It's gonna be *fine!"*

Jake didn't say much for a long time. Then he gave me a funny look and said in a quiet voice, "Well, maybe there's more to this miracle stuff than I thought."

I punched his arm and laughed right out loud. The coons and the varmints must have wondered what kind of animal had made *that* noise.

"It's gonna be better than *fine,* Joe. It's gonna be *wonderful!"*

16
A New Master Plan

BY the time we got back to Cedarville, it was almost ten in the morning. We were all so tired we were practically falling down. "Let's go to the sheriff's office and turn this crud over to him," I said.

On our way over there we noticed how deserted the streets were, but they always were on Sunday mornings. We went down Third Street. All the businesses were closed up. We headed toward Elm Street where the City Hall and jail were.

"What's that noise?" Joe asked. I could hear it, too.

"Isn't that music?" Jake said.

"Sounds like it. Let's stop and listen," I suggested. "It

couldn't be one of the churches, not in this part of town. Sounds like it's coming from City Hall."

"Oh, yeah," Jake said. "Coach said something about all the churches having a Christmas morning service at City Hall."

"You're right, Jake," I said. "Let's go in."

When we went into the building, we could hear everyone singing "O Little Town of Bethlehem." All the preachers were on the platform with a choir behind them. Christmas decorations were everywhere, and it was a pretty sight.

"Do you see the sheriff?" I whispered to Jake.

"There he is, over with the Assembly of God bunch." Jake opened his mouth to holler at him, but I shut him up.

"Quiet, you dingbat!" I said. "We don't want the whole town in on this!"

Well, whether we did or not, that's what we got.

Midnight must've caught a glimpse of Mr. Simmons, or maybe the singing inspired him. Anyway, that crazy dog gave a big lunge and dragged me right down toward the platform. He was crying as if he had the granddaddy of all boar coons up a gum stump. Midnight was a big dog, so pulling me along was about the same to him as pulling a bag of feathers.

Right then, Mr. Simmons jumped up and hollered, "That's my dog Midnight! I'd know that bark anywhere!"

Then he ran out of his row and met me and Midnight right in the middle of the Presbyterians! I don't think he even saw me. He was down on his knees, running his hands over that dog and talking to him as if he were a long-lost child. I looked up to see Sheriff Tanner wading through the Pentecostals to get to us. We all met right in the middle of the crowd. "Good to see you, boys!" Sheriff Tanner said.

"Got the dad-gummed old dognapper, Sheriff!" Joe hollered. "I laid him low with my good ol' Blasting Bolo!"

"This is the man who stole Mr. Simmons' dogs, Sheriff," I said. Everybody was real quiet. They were listening harder to me than to the preachers, I guess. "I don't know his name—"

"Well, *I* do!" Sheriff Tanner said. "Hello, Virgil. When did they let you out?"

"I ain't answerin' nothin' till I see a lawyer!"

"I bet," the sheriff grunted. "I ran Virgil outta the county two years ago for stealin' cows. He finally wound up in Cummins Prison for auto theft. What you been doing with the dogs, Virgil?"

"He told me he's been selling them to a laboratory in Oklahoma City," I put in. "He said he took them over by the truckload."

"Guess that'll be easy to check up on. Come on, Virgil. I'll get your cell ready." Then he turned to look at me, while he spoke to Virgil.

"By the way, why'd you leave two dogs when you took Midnight, Virgil? Not like you to leave anything."

Virgil shrugged. "I couldn't take 'em all. Had one dog already, and then this here boy, he tied the dogs to some trees. I seen him. I couldn't handle all them dogs. When I come back, both dogs were gone."

"Wait just a minute," the sheriff said slowly. *"Which* boy did you say? Was this the one?" He put his hand on my shoulder, and I held my breath.

Virgil scowled at me, shaking his head and pointing past me. "No, *that* one . . . with the red face!"

Everyone looked where Virgil was pointing. Bubba Simmons tried to hide behind his dad, but the sheriff was on him like a duck on a June bug. He collared him and pulled him out, then asked, "This the boy, Virgil?"

"I'll swear on a stack of Bibles," Virgil replied. "He's a pretty dumb kid to leave dogs tied up for me to steal!"

Things got real quiet all of a sudden. I felt sorry for Mr. Simmons. His usually red face turned pale as a sheet. His lips were trembling, and he could hardly talk. He went over to his son and after a few attempts managed to say, "Bubba? He's lying, isn't he, Son?"

But even Mr. Simmons could see Bubba was guilty. The kid started to shake and cry. "I didn't mean for it to happen—not the way it did. I was just mad at Barney because he beat my team in basketball! I was going to tell—honest I was."

Then the sheriff looked around at the whole town taking all this in, and I guess he must have felt sorry for the Simmonses, too. "Come on, Bubba, we'll have to talk about it. You come, too, Emmett. The rest of you go on with the service."

Everyone must've gotten out of the spirit of the celebration. One of the men, Mr. Pullen, asked if I had seen a black-and-tan hound with a white saddle.

"I saw him, Mr. Pullen," Jake answered. "He's out there, for sure."

"Where is he, boys?" Mr. Pullen shouted. "That's old Caravan or I'm a liar!"

About twenty of the men and some of the kids who had lost dogs all gathered around us and started asking if we'd seen this dog or that one. Then the sheriff said, "Pullen, you go see about the dogs, but I want a record of what dogs are there, you understand?"

"I'll take care of it. Where are they, Barney?" Mr. Pullen asked.

"Over close to Bandit Cave, about a quarter mile from the cave over in a bunch of hackberry trees. He's got the dogs in a big old barn."

"I know that place," Mr. Pullen said. Then turning to the group of men, he said, "Let's go, boys!"

His wife pulled at his sleeve. "You can't go until after the service!"

Suddenly the Baptist preacher popped up and said,

"I got to see if my Blue Wonder hound is there! I declare this service adjourned! Amen!" And the whole bunch disappeared quicker than you'd think possible! They left in a cloud of smoke from cars, pickups, and anything that would run.

Sheriff Tanner said to me, Jake, and Joe, "You come with me. Got to know a little more about this business." So we all went to the jail, and the wives and the kids of the men who'd left milled around, gossiping like mad.

There were so many folks following us to the jail that the sheriff had to weed a bunch out before we went inside.

Since there was still a bunch of people around, the sheriff nodded at me, and we went into the courtroom to get away from the crowd.

Mr. Simmons still had a bad color. His face was kinda yellow now, and he was breathing hard. His wife was standing by him holding his arm, and Debra was on the other side. Uncle Dave was over to his right, just watching. Bubba was sitting at one of the tables.

The sheriff looked at Mr. Simmons. "Emmett, you got anything to say?"

"I . . . I'm sorry about all this, Sheriff. I really thought the Buck boys took the dogs. Never would have thought a son of mine could be a dog thief!" Mr. Simmons loved dogs, and he loved his boy. Anyone who would steal a dog was low-down, but Bubba was still his boy. So Mr. Simmons had a real problem.

"You want to say anything about that reward?" Uncle Dave said loudly.

"Reward?" Mr. Simmons asked. "What reward?"

"The one you said last night you'd give to any man who found Midnight," Uncle Dave said. "A thousand dollars, wasn't it?"

Mr. Simmons looked at me, then said feebly, "Nobody heard me say that."

"*I* heard you!" Uncle Dave seemed to jump at his son. "Your wife and daughter heard you. Bubba heard you. I guess I'm waiting to see what sort of man I got for a son."

It got real quiet then, and finally Uncle Dave shook his head and looked right at Mr. Simmons. "You went wrong somewhere, Emmett. I've been watching you for a long time. Guess when you made your money, that's when you started to forget some things I tried to teach you. You were a good boy when you were young, and I was proud of you. Now look at you. Your word's no good. You don't have a real friend in the world. You've taught your boy to be a cheat and a thief. How far you plan to go with that kind of life?"

Mr. Simmons stood there taking it, and I never saw a man look so bad. He glanced at his family and didn't see much there to make him feel better. Then he lowered his head. "You're plumb right, Pa," he said in a choked-up voice. "I'm a mess. Have been for a long time, I guess. Somehow things got all . . . mixed up." He turned and went to stand by Bubba. "I've cheated you out of having a dad like the one I had. I sure am sorry, Bubba. You . . . you want to give me another chance?"

The next minute, the Simmons family was all huddled up, hugging one another. I was real glad for Debra and her mother—and for Bubba, too. He had been rotten, but who hasn't been at some time or another?

Finally Mr. Simmons came over and stuck his hand out. "Barney, I was wrong. Will you forgive me?"

Of course, he *had* been mean as a snake. But when I looked him in the eye, somehow I felt he was going to try to do better. I took his hand and nodded. "Why, shoot, yes, Mr. Simmons!" He shook my hand, then Jake's and Joe's.

He took a deep breath and looked at Uncle Dave, then back at us. "There's a balance of $2,220 on your place, boys," he said quietly. "As of this minute, I declare it paid in full. And it ain't charity, either. Midnight's worth ten times that." He stopped, all choked up again. "And so is my family's respect!"

"Whoopee!" Jake yelled, and we all did a little dance around the courtroom. I guess we deserved to celebrate, and everybody seemed to enjoy it.

I looked over toward the door and stopped my celebration. Miss Jean must have been there all the time, but I hadn't seen her. She was standing with Coach Littlejohn, just looking at the three of us. As soon as she saw I'd noticed her, she came toward me.

She wasn't wearing her nice smile. "Well, boys, you have anything you want to tell me?" When she stopped in front of me, I could swear she looked about as scary as Judge Poindexter had ever looked! My heart sank and I knew the jig was up. I glanced at Jake and Joe, and they looked as bad off as I felt.

"Well, Miss Jean, there's something I've been wanting to tell you for a long time."

"Yes, Barney?"

I figure Hitler probably looked more understanding than she did right then, but I'd started, so I decided to finish. "Well, the thing is, you know Uncle Roy and Aunt Ellen? Well, actually, the thing is, they never really did live here." She didn't say a word. "When we were about to get split up back in Chicago, well, we just about died. So we got this Master Plan about how we could stay together . . ."

Everybody was listening to me hard, which didn't make it any easier. It's bad enough I had to confess to lying and falsifying records and stuff, but to do it in front of all those people was real hard. Still, I tried to take the blame, because I was the oldest. Finally I came to the end of it.

"So that's what we did, and I'd like to tell you I wouldn't do it again, Miss Jean—"

She looked at me straight in the eye, and I shut my mouth. Then she said, "Do you mean that, Barney?"

All of a sudden I knew I did! It was hard to put into words, but I did the best I could. My face was probably as red as a beet.

"You see, Miss Jean, it's been bad, all the lies I had to tell the past few months. You didn't know our parents, but they brought us up to tell the truth, and a day hasn't passed since we started all this that I didn't think of Mom and Dad, you know? I mean, it was like I could see them, and they were real sad that we were lying to everybody."

"I see," she said in that soft voice of hers and reached out to put her arm around me. "And you wouldn't do it again, not even to stay together?"

"Well, I sure hope not! See, Miss Jean, Coach has been talking to me about what it means to be a Christian—and I think he's right about it. I mean, when you think about it, most all the people I trust generally turn out to be Christians, so I guess if I had it all to do over again, I'd like to believe that I'd just trust the Lord to help us without our doing a bunch of tricks."

"Well, *amen!*" Sheriff Tanner said. He wasn't the only

one who was looking pleased, either. Coach Littlejohn and Uncle Dave and several others looked like they could burst with their smiles!

I looked around and ended up by saying, "I'm really glad I don't have to lie anymore. I just want to be like Mom and Dad—and like you, Coach, and you, Sheriff Tanner. I just want to be *different.*"

Coach gave my arm a quick squeeze, then smiled over my head at Miss Jean. "I think we know what you're saying, Barney. I'm mighty proud of you."

"So am I," Jake said. He was standing next to me, and Joe was with him, and I just about lost it then. But I was the oldest, and it just wouldn't do for me to start blubbering in front of the whole town. So I put a hand on each of their shoulders, and my brothers and I turned to Miss Jean. She would have to have the final say in whatever became of us all. And this time we'd take it like men.

Miss Jean came over and hugged all three of us. "We'll have to get the record straight," she said firmly. "I can't let the court be misled."

Jake groaned. "That old Judge Poindexter will *kill* us!"

Miss Jean smiled. "Judge Poindexter retired last month. He's been replaced by Judge Elliot."

"He's probably *worse!*" Jake said gloomily.

"It's not a *he,* Jake. It's Judge Clara Elliot." She laughed. "Judge Elliot is much like a kind grandmother, which she is, by the way. We've talked about your case quite a bit. We're good friends."

"*How* good?" Jake demanded at once, and everyone laughed.

"Good enough that if I can give her a new Master Plan that will meet the standards of the law, I think there's a good chance you boys can continue to live here."

"Well, if it's money, I can help," Mr. Simmons said. I looked at him, startled, and so did Jake and Joe. *Whooee! Once miracles get started, they just don't stop!* I thought.

"Wonder if Judge Elliot would trust these boys to a small-town lawman?" Sheriff Tanner said.

But Coach Dale Littlejohn was louder than the others. "I really think what would impress the judge would be a couple. Say a small-town coach and a wife who's had lots of experience with boys."

If Emmett Simmons had had a red face, you should have seen Miss Jean right then! Everybody laughed. Then she walked right up to Coach and said in a good clear voice, "I've heard that southern men are long on flowery talk, but they can't follow through. Would you care to take a long walk and continue this line of conversation?"

Coach grinned sheepishly, then followed her out like he had a ring in his nose. Jake whooped and said, "Well, *he's* a goner!"

Mr. Simmons started to leave with his wife and Bubba, and I noticed that Uncle Dave was sticking close to Bubba. *That's all he's ever needed,* I thought. Even Bubba could change.

Then I felt a pull at my sleeve. It was Debra, and she was holding a big box wrapped in shiny green paper and topped by a big red bow. She handed it to me. "It's your Christmas present, Barney. I left it here with the sheriff to give to you."

I felt foolish. "Shoot, Debra! I feel bad. I didn't get you a thing."

She gave me one of those heavy-lidded looks of hers that always made me uncomfortable, then tapped her lower lip with her fingertip. Then she said in that sort of innocent way she has, "Oh, well, maybe we can think of *something* you can give me."

"Go on, Barney," Joe urged. "Open it."

I removed the paper carefully and opened the box. When I looked inside, I didn't dare look up—not for a minute. I knew I was expected to say something, but I first had to swallow the lump in my throat.

"What is it?" Jake asked. "Let's have a look."

I took the gift out of the box, cleared my throat, then said, "It's . . . it's a wheat light."

"What's *that?"* Joe asked.

"It's a headlight with a power source that you carry on your belt." I could have told them all about this one, because I'd carried the ad from the *American Cooner* for a long time. I'd been using an old carbide lamp that was good for one thing: going out when I needed it most!

Debra must have seen me looking at that ad, then gotten the headlight on the sly.

Finally, I looked directly into her eyes. "Maybe you'd like to go out tonight and see how it works?"

"But you been up half the night," Joe piped up. "You'll be too tired!"

I gave Debra a look. "Nope. I don't think I will."

Jake and Joe just groaned, then came to hug me and slap me on the back. I grinned at them and at Debra, and we all started to leave the courtroom. "Well, it looks like the Bucks of Goober Holler are safe at last," I said. "Now if we can just stay out of trouble—"

Jake suddenly grabbed me by the arm. He had that look on his face. You know, the one that usually meant trouble—for me!

"There's something I've been wanting to tell you, Barney." His eyes got bright, and I felt myself slipping under his power as he pulled me close and whispered confidentially, "Just wait till you hear my latest plan!"

Nicky Fifth's How to Train Your Government

To all of the kids who now carry the burden of governing and untangling the mess left by former generations. If you enjoy your freedoms, you must find a way to get citizens to plug into government and civics. If you don't enjoy your freedoms, watch the evening news to see the alternatives.

~LFW

In memory of Linda Martins, an advocate for children and an example for all.

Franklin Mason Press
ISBN 978-0-9857218-7-9
Library of Congress Control Number: 2017951800

Printed and Published in the United States of America

Cover illustrations by Lauren Lambiase

Cover design by Monica Thomas, TLC Graphics, *www.tlcgraphics.com*

Editorial and Production Staff:
Jennifer Wahner, Iris Hutchinson, Allyssa Barnes, Susan Masterpole, Amanda Tenzer, Reynold Funari, Lorraine Funari

www.franklinmasonpress.com
www.nickyfifth.com

Nicky Fifth's

How to Train Your Government

by Lisa Funari-Willever

Franklin Mason Press
COLUMBUS, NEW JERSEY

E PLURIBUS UNUM

Table of Contents

This is the United States Flag outside the Capitol Building in Washington DC.

Introduction

Hi, my name is **Nicky Fifth** and this is **T-Bone** and **Wanda**.

You might be wondering why a few kids want to talk **politics**. That's a good question, but the answer is simple; we love history, civics, and, believe it or not, even politics. When T-Bone ran for student council president, I was his **campaign manager**. And the person he ran against? You guessed it...Wanda. Yup, my best friend and some girl who once drove me crazy, ran against each other.

And how did that election turn out, you ask? Let's just say it didn't end the way I imagined it would end. **I thought T-Bone would win** in a landslide, but it was close. It was so close that the winner decided to share the presidency with the runner-up. I know, I know, you're still wondering who won. Add that to the list of **life's great mysteries**. Personally, I think my best friend, T-Bone, who's had a major crush on Wanda since the day she first insulted him, won the election. My evidence? Well, every time I asked him if he won, he talked about how great her hair smelled. Not the best proof in the world, I know, but definitely suspicious.

So, you're looking to **train your government?** That's awesome. It's a good idea, even though some people say it would be easier to teach an elephant to balance on a ball.

WAIT! STOP! Do not put the book down!

Think about it. A lot of things in life are hard. Solving a Rubik's Cube blindfolded? Hard. Hiking the Appalachian Trail? Very hard. Walking on a tight rope? Nearly impossible. And walking on a tightrope while solving a Rubik's cube blindfolded? Don't even get me started.

That's okay. **Don't be afraid** of difficult. **Don't run away** when something's hard. Face challenges head on, try to understand them, and then … drumroll please … **just come up with a strategy**. Yup, it's that easy: face it, understand it, and then plan your strategy.

And, don't worry because this book will show you, step-by-step, how to train your government. And, spoiler alert … **it's not nearly as complicated as you might think**.

★ CHAPTER ONE ★

Figure Out What a Government Actually Is

Sure, we've all heard the word **government**. In fact, we hear it all the time. It's in the news every single day. Your family probably complains about it. Your neighbors complain about it. If your pets could, they'd probably complain about it, too. But what is this thing called government and **why do people always sound so mad at it?**

The first definition in the dictionary says: government is the act of governing. Hmmm. Not very helpful using the word in the definition.

Let's try a different definition right out of kidsbritanica.com: *Any group of people living together in a country, state, city, or local community has to live by certain rules. The* **system of rules**, *and the* **people who make and administer them**, *are known as a government.*

That's more like it.

So, the people who **create the rules** by which we live are the government. And, the people who **decide if those laws are fair** are the government. And, the **people who enforce those laws are** also the government. But, how do we know what people in the government do? Sometimes, it seems like a private club and only a few people know the secret knock. You might even be wondering what to call these government people. Governeers? Govies? Governmenters?

Don't worry. There are names for everyone in government and those names are usually **based upon their jobs**. If you're a lawmaker, guess what your job is?

Yup, you guessed it, you make the laws. Just like a shoemaker makes shoes, **a lawmaker makes laws**.

If you're a kid, you probably don't have a lot of experience making laws, or even rules. For most of your life, someone has probably told you what to wear and what not to wear, what to eat and what not to eat, when to sleep, when to wake up, and even when to talk or be quiet. That's a lot of rules that **you're not making**.

I know what you're thinking—**HOLY MOLY**, my parents must be in the government. No one makes more rules than my parents! Not only do they make important rules and safety rules, sometimes, I think, they make rules just for fun.

Don't worry, understanding the jobs of the government isn't super complicated. In fact, the explanation involves **a tree**. Yup, you read that correctly, a tree. You may be wondering, why a tree? Is it because trees have deep roots, provide things like air, fruit and shade, or because they're a symbol of strength and longevity? Nope. It's because **they have branches!** Yup, it turns out branches do more than hold nests, ornaments, and tree swings. A tree's branches are a wonderful way to **show how the government is divided**.

Now, before we go any further, you should know that **not every country** divides the powers of government. There are countries that give all the power to one person. In those cases, training the government is impossible because no one really has a voice. Dozens of countries are **ruled by dictators** and their citizens cannot enjoy the many freedoms our constitution guarantees our citizens. That's why it's so important to not only use your voice, but to appreciate the fact that you're allowed to have one. **So, don't waste it**.

Back to the tree. Tree sounds kind of boring so let's call it the…

Yes, that's much better than plain old tree. In the United States, there are three main branches that emerge from the trunk of the Tree of Democracy: the **Executive Branch**, the **Legislative Branch**, and the **Judicial Branch**.

For the **Federal Government**, which is what we call the United States Government, the **Executive Branch** would be the President. See, you just learned another name for the President: Executive Branch. Want to know the acronym for the President of the United States? You guessed it, it's **POTUS**. Now, when you hear that term on the news, you'll know exactly who it means. And, if you hear the term **FLOTUS**, that's the president's wife, or the First Lady.

The next branch is the **Legislative Branch** which is the lawmakers. Before you get confused, legislate means to make laws, so the legislative branch is the people who make our laws. This branch is divided into **two houses, or chambers**, of lawmakers, called the **Senate** and the **House of Representatives**. Together, they form our Congress, or the 535 people who represent the citizens and the states. Sorry, no fun acronym for this group.

Finally, the third branch is the **Judicial Branch**. The word judicial means something that's related to a judge or courts. For this branch, it's the Supreme Court of the United States, or if you'd like another fun acronym, **SCOTUS**. The Supreme Court judges are called **Justices** and there are nine of them. **Why nine**, you ask? Do they have a baseball team? Nope! Believe it or not, there's actually no constitutional rule regarding how many justices are required. It has changed often, but since the Judiciary Act of 1869, we have had nine.

The three main branches each have **specific duties**, but, technically, they are all **equal**.

WHAT? How can they all be equal? Everyone knows the President has more power, **right?**

Not right. Over the years, people just assumed the president had the most power. But, as powerful as you believe the president is, the other branches have the same amount of power.

Thanks to the wisdom of our Founding Fathers, **Checks and Balances** prevent one branch of government from becoming more powerful than the other two branches. Each branch has the power to check and then balance the other powers.

Dividing up the power was one of the most brilliant ideas our **Founding Fathers'** included when they were forming our government. Three branches of government, **all separate, but all equal**. Are you wondering what made them think of three co-equal branches?

That one's easy. His name: **King George III**. Having been ruled by a British King, the Founding Fathers wanted to form a nation that prevented one person from having **absolute rule** and to **protect the rights of the citizens.**

You may be wondering **why we even need a government**, especially after we fought a revolution to rid ourselves of our government. You must, however, remember that we were British subjects at the time. We fought a revolution to rid ourselves of **a tyrannical King** and occupation by British soldiers.

That brings us to another important point: our Founding Fathers never believed that we didn't need a government. They knew **government was important** and that a country without a government would be a **total mess**. They believed in a government that was of the people, by the people, and for the people.

So, **why, exactly, do we need a government?** As a civilized society, we sometimes lose sight of the things that make our lives so civilized. Do you like to go places? Government builds and maintains roads. Do you like safety? Our country is protected by the military, our waters are protected by the Coast Guard and our lives, homes, and properties are protected by police and firefighters. People often get so mad at the government that **they forget how much the government provides**. From streets to schools and everything in between, our government impacts all of our lives.

Since every country is different, you may be wondering just what *our* government does. Wanda searched several websites and learned that the list of government services is long. And this isn't everything.

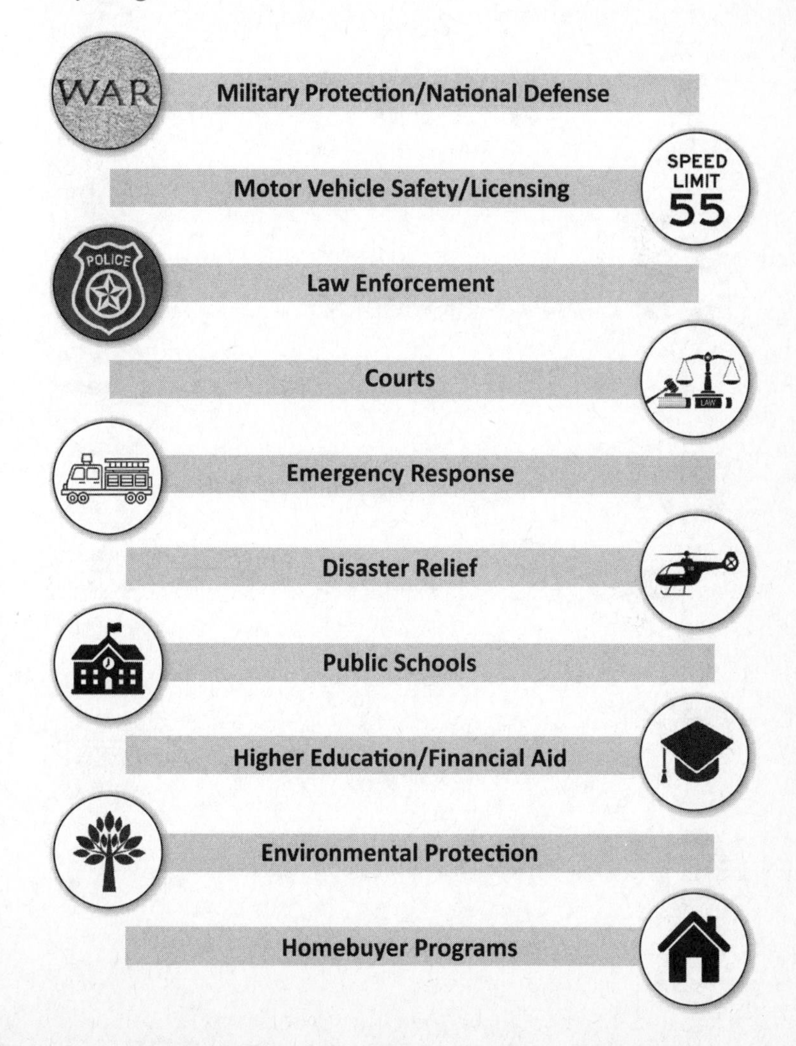

Programs for Senior Citizens

Programs for the Disabled

Programs for Babies and Children

Programs for Poverty

Foreign Relations

Transportation Safety

Food Protection

Libraries

Medical Research

Highways

Trade with Other Countries

Consumer Protection
Museums and Historic Sites
MUSEUM
Postal Services
MAIL
National, State, & Local Parks
Business & Banking Regulations
Weather Alerts
PBS (Public Broadcasting)
Prisons and Jails
Energy Management
NASA—Space Exploration
Medicare and Medicaid

That isn't even everything! Can you imagine life without all of those things? People get mad at it, but without the government, our lives would look **much different**.

So, now you're probably really confused. We get it and we know what you're thinking. If the government provides so many things to so many people, **why is everyone always so mad at it?** That's a good question. There are lots of reasons that people become irritated with the government. Remember, it's not perfect, so train it.

Some people are just always mad at certain lawmakers, or the President, or the Supreme Court. Some people just get mad about specific issues. Then there are some people, and we're not sure why, who are always mad at everything. This, of course, doesn't count the people who are happy and the people who choose to not even pay attention.

Think about it this way. We're lucky enough to have a government that is of the people, by the people, and for the people. **Did you see that?** The word **people** pops up three times. That's right. **People**. The government isn't just the people we elect and appoint. The government is the people and that's **all of us**.

We, the people, are called **constituents** and our role is even **more important** than the people we elect and the people they appoint. If we, collectively, fail to do our jobs, how can we expect the people we elect to do theirs?

The next time you hear someone complaining, ask them **how often they communicate** with their elected officials, you know, calls, letters, meetings. Find out if they always pay attention or if they only show up when an issue affects them.

Tip from T-Bone

No one expects you to **love every decision** the government makes. In fact, that's what makes our democracy so special. You don't have to love it and, in America, you don't even have to pretend to love it.

But, as Americans, we don't just have the option to use our voices, we have **a responsibility to use our voices**. That's because **we** are part of the government. In fact, **we** are the most important part of the government.

Think about it. We have almost **330 million citizens**. In the federal government, there are only **545 individuals** who make and enforce the laws that we all live by.

Unless they are the absolute quietest people in the world, nearly 330 million voices **should be louder** than a mere 545 people.

If you're thinking of running for office, check out the salaries of these elected officials.

Salaries of Government Officials

as of 2017

President of the United States	$400,000
Vice President	$230,700
Speaker of the House	$223,500
House Majority/Minority Leader	$193,400
Senate Members	$174,000
House of Representative Members	$174,000
Chief Justice, Supreme Court	$258,100
Associate Justices, Supreme Court	$246,800

To put these numbers in perspective, according to the Bureau of Labor Statistics, the median wage for workers in the United States in the fourth quarter of 2016 was $849 per week or $44,148 per year for a 40-hour work week.

CHAPTER TWO

Count Your Governments

Count our governments? Hold on!
More than one government? What? How can that can be?

Okay, you may want to sit down for this one. Each citizen has **several governments**. And, to train them, you better know them. Yes, there's the federal government, but there's also state, county, and local governments, boards, and commissions.

STOP! DON'T PUT THE BOOK DOWN! DEEP BREATHS!

It's not complicated. Especially if you know how to use the *Tree of Democracy*.

State government is **very similar** to the federal government, except the Executive Branch has a governor instead of a president. The Legislative Branch still has lawmakers, and each state has a Supreme Court.

Federal		State
President	**Executive**	Governor
Lawmaker	**Legislative**	Lawmaker
Supreme Court	**Judicial**	Supreme Court

Your state is divided into **areas called districts** and each district has representatives on the legislative branch. Where you live determines your district.

In New Jersey, the two houses of lawmakers are called the **Assembly** and the **Senate**.

In Pennsylvania, the **Senate** and **House of Representatives** make up the General Assembly.

In California, the **Senate** and **Assembly** make up the California State Legislature.

The Michigan State Legislature is made up of a **Senate** and a **House of Representatives**.

Bicameral

Except for Nebraska, every state legislature is called *bicameral.* That simply means that they have **two houses, or chambers, of lawmakers**: an upper house and a lower house.

In Nebraska, it's what they call unicameral. That means there's only one house. In Nebraska, that one house is the Senate.

You're probably asking yourself…if we're all part of one country, why does every state have a different form of state government?

That's easy. Refer to **King George III**. Remember, he's the reason we wanted a democracy and freedoms. Even though the original 13 colonies wanted to become a united country, they weren't interested in handing over all of their powers to a federal government or each other.

They also had **major concerns**. Northern states wanted to make sure Southern states didn't boss them around and Southern states wanted to make sure Northern states didn't boss them around. The Southern states were larger, but the northern states had more people.

After the Revolution, when the thirteen colonies decided to join together and form **one nation**, they needed to decide what rights belonged to the United States government and which ones belonged to the states.

As a result, the **states' rights** issue was born. You would think, in over 200 years, this issue would be completely and finally settled, and for the most part, it is. But, even now, there are conflicts between the rights of the federal government and the state governments.

From the very beginning, states were concerned about their level of representation. It was very hard to come up with one formula that fairly represented everyone. Of course, **larger states** with high populations preferred the number of representatives each state received to be **based upon population**. In that scenario, states with the most people would get the most votes and, ultimately, have the most control.

As you can imagine, **smaller states** and those with less people prefered that each state had the **same amount** of representatives to keep things even. *Thank goodness for compromises!*

The House of Representatives

Since good government relies on compromise, a compromise, of sorts, was born. It was a two house, or two chamber, solution. The House of Representatives, the lower house, is based upon population. **In low-population states**, like Alaska and Delaware, each state receives **one representative**.

HOLD ON! We know what you're wondering. Why does the biggest state and one of the smallest states get the same amount? That's easy. Remember, the amount of representatives each state gets is based upon population, or how many people live there.

It has nothing to do with the size of the land. **This is based upon number of people, not square miles**.

The Connecticut Compromise of 1787

Believe it or not, at the 1787 Constitutional Convention, there was a disagreement over whether representatives should serve one-year terms or three-year terms. The result was a compromise with two-year terms!

And, if you're wondering how a state as big as Alaska can have a population similar to that of little old Delaware, that's easy, too. Much of Alaska is a rugged frontier with lots and lots of open space and it's a challenging place to live. In fact, here's the list of states that have only **one representative** in the House of Representatives:

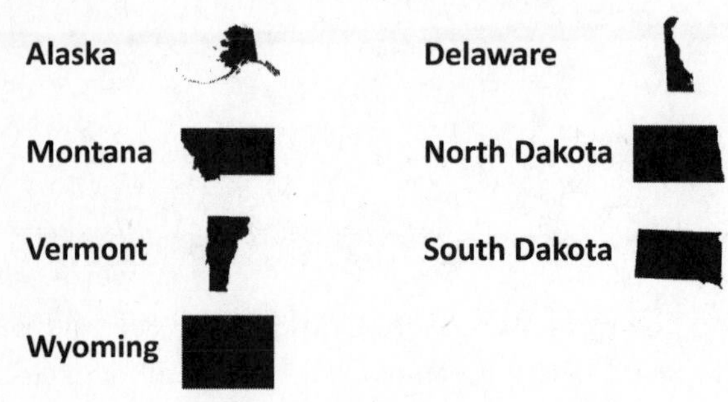

Of course, some states have **much higher numbers**:

California	53	Florida	27
Texas	36	New York	27
Illinois	18	Pennsylvania	18
Michigan	14	North Carolina	13
Ohio	16	Georgia	14
New Jersey	12	Virginia	11

Since each state is **divided into districts**, citizens can only vote for the candidate in their district. The only time a whole state votes for the same candidates is when that state has only one representative. Everyone else votes for the one seat in their district.

Whether your state has one representative or fifty-three, one thing is the same and that is **the term**. The term is the amount of time a representative serves. And, for the House of Representatives, **the term is two years**.

Yes, you read that right. Most people assume it's a four-year term, like the presidency. This was a compromise by our Founding Fathers and it's still a point that **many people disagree** with.

Independence Hall
Philadelphia, PA

Those who support two-year terms say that it gives voters a chance to remove a representative if they notice they are not performing as promised. Our Founding Fathers believed this would be a **guard against tyranny**. It also took into account the distances many early representatives traveled without the luxury of trains, planes, and automobiles.

The framers of the constitution also felt that short terms would force members to interact with their constituents more frequently.

Those who disagree with the two-year terms state that as soon as a representative is elected, their decisions are often based upon **getting re-elected**. They also believe that short terms mean representatives spend a whole lot of time **fundraising and campaigning** and less time governing. For representatives, it must feel like a never ending campaign season.

So, what goes on over at the other house?

The Senate

The Upper House of the Federal Legislative branch is called the Senate. Unlike the House of Representatives, **every state has two senators**. Yup, that's it. No fooling around with this one. You get two, and you get two, and you get…I think you see where we're going with this.

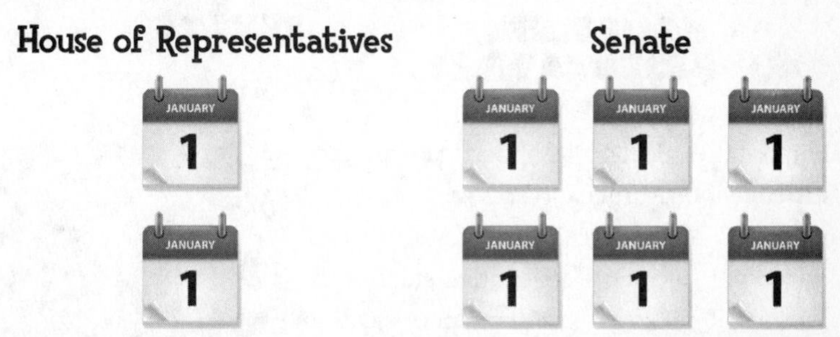

Now, number of representatives isn't the only difference. Another difference from the House is the length of the term. While the House serves two years and the President and Vice President serve four years, the term for a United States Senator is **a whole whopping six years**. And to avoid turmoil, every two years, one third of the Senate is up for election. By staggering the elections, the country would always have some stability.

Now that you know about **the two chambers** of the legislative branch, you're probably asking yourself the following question:

Besides the number of lawmakers and length of their terms, what's the difference?

Well, the legislative branch is called **Congress** and we know that Congress is broken into two houses, the Senate and the House of Representatives. Together, they write and vote on bills or new laws, and divide the work into committees.

The Senate, alone, has special **powers to approve** Supreme Court Justices and members of the President's Cabinet, you know, the people whose titles start with *Secretary*. The Vice President serves as the President of the Senate and is called upon when a tie needs to be broken.

The House of Representatives is the only chamber that can introduce **spending bills**. They also reserve the right to initiate any **impeachment proceedings**.

Your State Government

Phew! Congratulations on understanding the federal government, but don't celebrate yet! Now, it's time to figure out state government.

You're lucky, most state governments are **modeled after the federal government**. Training a state government won't be much different than training the federal government. You have the same three branches, and except for Nebraska, they are all bicameral. The only difference is the names for each chamber.

Some states use Senate or State Senate. Some use Assembly, General Assembly, House of Representatives, House of Delegates, or State Assembly. All you really need to know is what your state uses and that, with the exception of Nebraska, each state has **an upper and a lower house, or chamber**.

We know what you're thinking. Why do we need two, almost identical governments? Ah, but **they're not identical**. Remember the state's rights issue we talked about earlier? Well, that's why! Some items are decided by the federal government, while others are a state's responsibility.

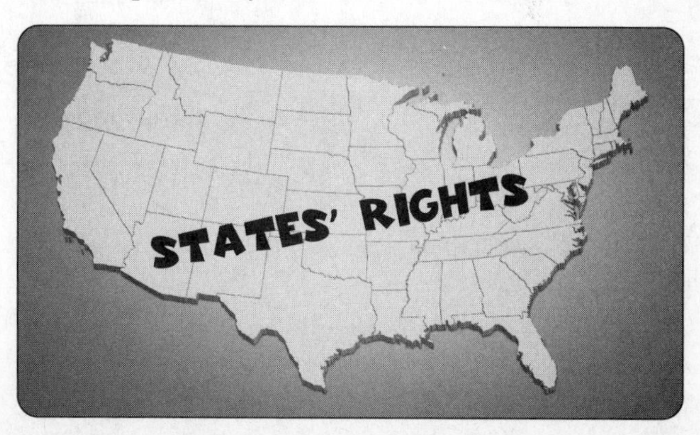

In a perfect world, everyone would know exactly which rights and responsibilities belonged to the federal government and which belonged to state governments.

Unfortunately, it's not always that easy. Over the years, there have been conflicts over who is responsible for what. So, what are the duties, rights and responsibilities of both governments?

Federalism—established since the signing of the Constitution, federalism is the sharing of powers between both the national and individual state governments.

Earlier, we learned about many of the jobs assigned to the federal government. Below is a list of important **federal powers**:

Make money

Make and Enforce Laws

Declare War

Make Taxes

Manage Foreign Relations

Borrow Money

Trade with Other Countries

Below is a list of **state powers**:

Ratify Amendments

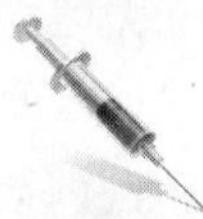

Manage Public Health & Safety

Oversee In-state Trade

Make and Enforce Laws

Make Taxes

Borrow Money

So, you want to be a lawmaker?

Requirements to be a:

Representative	Senator
25 years of age	30 years of age
Citizen for at least 7 years	Citizen for at least 9 years
Resident of the state	Resident of the state

The Good News, Bad News Scenario

So, we'll give you the good news first: learning about Federal and State governments is pretty easy because they're very similar.

Now, for the bad news. There are **lots and lots of other forms of government** and they range from familiar to wacky! The reason they are so different is that they are more local.

From counties and parishes to cities and towns to commissions and boards, local government becomes very interesting. Let's start with **County Government**. A county is a region of a state that includes smaller cities and towns. Counties have borders and almost every state has them. See? This is where it gets interesting!

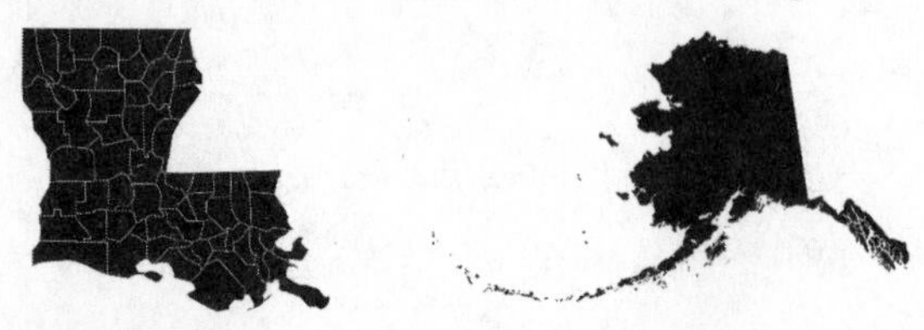

Louisiana and Alaska have **parishes** instead of counties.

Connecticut and Rhode Island counties have **NO government**.

From state to state, the power of county government varies wildly. From simple boundaries in some states to handling major functions in other states, **the level of power is never the same**.

In some states, there are county school districts, county emergency services such as firefighters and paramedics, and county law enforcement. In other states, counties provide court services, election services, vital statistics (like your birth certificate), and sometimes libraries, hospitals, and parks. **It's always different.**

In some states, if you need a copy of your birth certificate, you go to the county building. When you put out your trash or recycling cans, in many states, the county picks them up.

And who leads the county? Well, there's usually **an elected body** which means a group of people that must be elected for a specific term. Sometimes this group is called a Board of Freeholders, a Board of Chosen Freeholders, a County Commission, a Board of Supervisors, or even a County Council.

The day-to-day activities in a county are often handled by the **County Executive or County Administrator**. Many counties also have a County Clerk, a County Treasurer, a County Surrogate, and a County Sheriff.

So far, we have the Federal government, State governments, and County governments. What else is left?

Now, it's time to talk **local government**. Think city hall or town hall. How much power the city or town has depends upon how much power the county has. From big cities to small towns, each situation is unique. Many cities and towns have **elected mayors** while smaller ones have managers, or are led by the county. The people who govern the city, town, borough, or village are often elected officials that make up a governing council.

Besides cities, towns, boroughs, and villages, local government comes in many forms, including school districts, fire districts, commissions, and boards. Some are very public and open with their work, while **some are less open**. In fact, many citizens have no idea that these organizations exist. More importantly, many citizens don't know that these groups have the **power to levy taxes**. Yup-taxes!

There are so many forms of government that affect so many parts of our lives. Not knowing who they are or what they do could be a very big and very expensive mistake. Do yourself a favor and figure out what they do.

CHAPTER THREE

How This Whole Government Thing Works

T-Bone here! My friend, Nick, did a good job explaining exactly what government is, but now I'm going to tell you the **inside story**. Like most things in life, politics and government are not always what you see. **You didn't see that one coming, did you?**

Let's start at the beginning—campaigns. In politics, the campaign is your **work and effort to get elected**. The amount of time a campaign lasts depends upon the office you're seeking. Generally speaking, the larger the office, the longer the campaign.

If you decide that you want to **step up and take a stand on issues**, then running for office might be for you. Even if you're not the type to run for office, **you should still know how this all works**; and more importantly, how it is **supposed to work**.

DON'T CHANGE A THING
CHANGE EVERYTHING

How a Campaign *Should* Start

Say you have some great ideas and you decide to run for mayor of a small town. **In a perfect world**, your campaign would start this way:

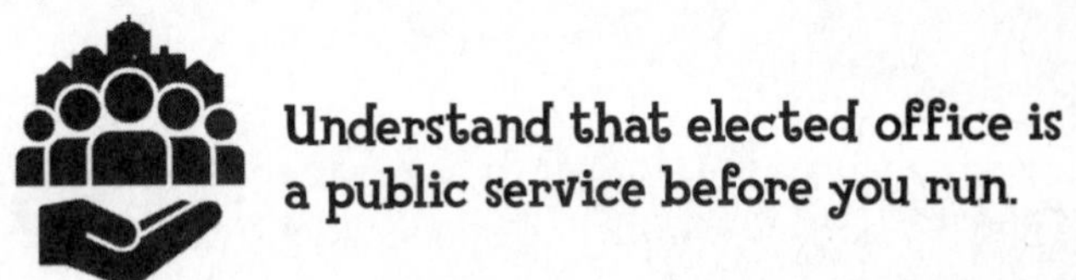

Understand that elected office is a public service before you run.

Yup, that's right, it's service. Give it a lot of thought. **Seriously**, give it some real hard thought. You can't imagine how much time and effort comes with an elected office. Don't underestimate how much work is involved. And, it's not just the work to get elected. If you're elected, **the work required to serve the people** is very demanding. Make sure your family is on board and you know what you're getting into.

Figure out the money.

It takes **a lot of money** to run a campaign. Find out if your political party (Democrat, Republican, Libertarian, etc.) is willing to support your efforts. They may be able to provide you with some money. Also, check your own finances to see what you can afford to contribute while asking **friends and family** if they would be willing to donate.

Find smart people to work on your campaign.

You'll need a **campaign manager** to run everything for you. When I ran against Wanda for Student Council, Nicky was my manager. Most campaigns will also have someone who manages your schedule, someone who manages the money, someone who manages the media, and even someone who manages your volunteers. Even though Nicky did all of those jobs for me, **avoid picking friends or family** for these roles. They make great volunteers and cheerleaders, but if they don't have a background in politics, you could have many, many headaches.

Decide where you stand.

Wanting to run is a good first step, but if you don't know the issues inside and out, and if you don't have good ideas, you should **rethink the whole idea**. If you decide to continue, it's time to research issues and solutions. Now, this doesn't mean to look up one story or read a couple of headlines. This means relying on several sources from different points of view and following the issues. The goal is to have **a well-rounded understanding** of the issues so, if you get elected, you can get right to work.

Figure out where your opponent stands.

In a campaign, you should **know where your opponent stands**. Keep in mind, there may actually be places where you both agree. Don't disagree just to be different. Point out where you agree and be able to thoroughly explain where you disagree by using facts. A smart candidate will research an opponent's positions and actions related to issues and avoid digging up personal information on an opponent's family or personal life. **Stick to the issues**.

Create your brand.

When you hear the word brand, you probably think of **products** like cereal and laundry detergent; but as a candidate, you will need a brand, too. Your brand should be based upon **your ideas and positions**. Perhaps your brand is clean energy or education or fighting crime. Whatever your focus is, that will become your brand. Once you have a brand you can create a catchy slogan and order things like signs and postcards. Just remember, your brand should **reflect you and your beliefs**.

Get to work.

The next step is called **getting to work**. That means going to meetings, writing letters to the editor, participating in debates, knocking on doors (always with your team, never alone), mailing information, and using the internet and social media to spread your message. The goal is to let people meet you and see what you're all about. This is the time to **be genuine and be yourself**. Not everyone will agree with you, and that's okay as long as you take the high road. And the good news…the high road never has any traffic!

If you get elected...

If you get elected, you'll now be responsible for **your words and actions**, for the issues you support and for those that you don't. Whether you're elected to represent your school district, your town, your county, your state, or the entire country, **you are not there to represent yourself**. You are the **voice of the people** you represent. Never, for even a moment, believe that you are irreplaceable or that your needs are more important than those you represent.

Average Length of Campaigns Around the World

Presidential, Prime Minister, Leader Campaigns

USA	596 days
Great Britain	30 days
Germany	42 days
Australia	56 days
Canada	Less than 10-weeks
Mexico	Less than 147 days
Japan	12 days

Electoral college what?

Both words sound important...**electoral** and **college**. Put them together and they sound twice as important. But honestly, what the heck does **electoral college** even mean?

You may wanna sit down for this one. First of all, the electoral college **isn't a place** or an actual college! Yup, no classrooms, no books, no professors, not even a football team.

So what is it? It's actually a group of people called **electors**. Each state automatically gets two, which is **one for every Senator**. The remaining electors are based upon how many representatives each state has, which we know is **based upon population**.

So, now you're wondering what they do. Well, they actually **elect the President of the United States**. What??? Yup, they elect the president. How is that fair? Well, the electors, who are usually state-elected officials, party leaders, or people with a connection to the Presidential candidates, are usually picked at the state convention. Except for two states, Nebraska and Maine, all of a states electors must go to the candidate that wins that state's **popular vote**.

Wondering what the popular vote is? That's the votes of all of the individual registered voters. In recent elections, the candidate who won the popular vote actually **lost the election** because of the electoral college. The **total number of electors is 538** and the candidate who reaches **270 wins**. Visit nickyfifth.com for a cool slide show that explains it with pictures!

How Lots of Campaigns *Really* Start

Hi, this is Wanda and I know a little bit about close campaigns and elections. I also know that while we have **a lot of decent and dedicated politicians**, there are those who are less decent and dedicated.

Now that T-Bone has told you how a campaign **should** start, let's see **how lots of campaigns actually start.**

We know that, in the beginning, many people enter politics with the **best of intentions**. Somewhere along the way, however, many politicians become **blinded by power and greed**.

Remember the part that said an elected office is a **public service?** Well, not everyone sees it that way. Sadly, there are some elected officials that are only there for their own interests.

How can someone benefit from being an elected official?

Being an elected official technically makes you a public servant. Yup, doesn't sound very glamorous, does it? But, don't let the name fool you. **Think about it**. Elected officials make laws, they have influence, and they have power. The higher the office, the more power they have. So, how do they turn their power into something valuable?

The first thing you need to know about: **Special Interests**. They sound innocent enough, but **not all special interests are alike**. Special interests are groups of people that share a common interest. One person could be a part of many, many special interest groups and many do great work.

An organization that protects water is interested in clean water. A power company is interested in things like electricity. An organization of doctors will be interested in health issues.

Being part of a special interest group is not a problem. Over the years, special interests have fought for things like veterans, equal rights, child labor laws, and public safety. Those are great causes and people who believed in them worked together to rally public support. For special interest groups, one way to support a cause **is to lobby**.

Yes, you read that right, the activity is called **lobbying** and the person doing it is the **lobbyist**. One old story claims the word was used by President Ulysses S. Grant. He used the term to refer to people who would hang in the Willard Hotel lobby, in Washington DC, **hoping to speak to him and influence his decisions**.

So, if lobbying is the act of **influencing someone's thoughts and actions**, it must be **pretty bad, right?** Not so fast! **It all depends**.

If you belong to a group that wants to see safer playgrounds, your group might hire a lobbyist. This person would research and gather information, make phone calls, and create a strategy. Part of that strategy would be to **reach out to lawmakers** and share that information with them.

In that case, a lobbyist is a useful tool for achieving a worthy goal. What if, however, you are a food manufacturer and you want to keep the food label measurements in metric so no one in the United States could really understand what was in your foods? That's not a worthy goal and because of that, the lobbyists might need to get **very creative**. To persuade, they could take the politician to fancy events and restaurants, or even golfing at expensive golf courses. The biggest thing they can do, however, is to **donate money to their campaigns**.

Yes, campaigns need money, lots of money. The higher the office, the more money they need. Lobbyists know that politicians spend a great deal of time raising money. **To get their attention and support, lobbyists donate money**.

HOLD ON! Yes, I know what you're thinking. That **sounds a lot like bribery**. Well, yes, it does sound like it. Someone wants a politician to do something and they donate a lot of money. Then the politician does it. Sounds a lot like **buying a vote**.

This is an enormous problem. If you ever hear the words **campaign finance reform** when you're watching the news, this is one of the things they're talking about. Here's an example:

A company wants to put ads for cotton candy inside school buses, but they know most parents would be against that idea.

They hire a lobbyist to represent their **special interest**.

The lobbyist takes some lawmakers to lunch and explains that selling the ads will raise a lot of money. They even discuss **campaign donations**.

Parents find out and get very **angry**. They don't want posters that promote **unhealthy** food choices inside of the school buses and start calling the same lawmakers.

The problem:

The lawmakers are getting phone calls from the **lobbyist and the parents**. Soon, they will **have to vote** on this issue.

How do you think they will vote?

Now, what if the cotton candy company **gives the lobbyist money** to donate to the their campaign?

Now, how do you think the politician will vote?

Part of the problem may be that campaigns in America take **too, too long**.

Part of the problem may be that our campaigns have become much **too expensive**.

And of course, a big part of the problem is that some special interests **use money to control how some politicians vote**.

We Know...You have a lot of questions!

How can that be **legal?**

How can that be **fair?**

Why would someone who **takes an oath**
to serve the people **vote for bad ideas?**

Why do these politicians **need the money so badly?**

When politicians who vote for things that benefit them
or their donors, do they know **that it's wrong?**

All good questions. Here are some **honest answers**. In most cases, it's legal, but only because the laws for campaign donations are **way too loose**. That's not to say that there haven't been actual bribery cases, because there have been plenty.

From local government to higher offices, many people have been caught and sent to prison for things like bribery and corruption. In most cases, people **start off good** and do not intend to abuse the power of their office.

But, too often, they get caught up in **the power** of holding an elected office. They like it so much, that they want to **keep getting re-elected**. And **that takes money**.

Often, without that money, they cannot get re-elected. Too avoid feeling bad, they do something called **rationalize**. That means they talk themselves into believing something they know may not be correct, **but that they wish to be true**.

They tell themselves that they are doing such good and important work that **it would hurt people if they weren't there to do it**. Then they **rationalize EXACTLY why it's okay** to make decisions that benefit themselves.

Go back to the candy-posters-in-the-bus example. Some of the parents who are complaining may make small donations while others don't donate at all. They're **all constituents**, but they're **not all supporters**.

The candy company, as the lobbyist promised, makes a single $100,000 donation.

Who usually gets the lawmaker's attention?

Right now, you're probably **a little shocked**. But, wait, there's more. Have you ever heard of the term **rider?** Of course you have! There's bike rider, bus rider, car rider…

Actually, that's a different rider and not the rider that affects everyone's life. **This rider is a bill**. Not a grocery bill or credit card bill, but **an idea before it becomes a law**.

Suppose you're the politician who is writing the bill to allow cotton candy posters inside school buses. A lot of parents have been making a fuss against the idea, but the candy company has contributed $100,000 to your campaign fund. Now, **you have to convince the other lawmakers** to vote yes for the bill. But that could be a problem.

Other lawmakers **may not want to vote for your bill**. They might consider it too risky. Plus, **no one gave them $100,000** to vote for it. So how do you get their support?

One way is to add a rider, or another bill, to your bill. It doesn't even have to be related to your bill. Just any bill that you know another lawmaker would like to pass. And, it doesn't have to be just one rider.

If you **attach enough of your colleagues' bills** to your bill, you may get enough votes. Now, everyone who votes for your bill is voting for twelve other bills. And, because they're attached, you either **vote for all of them or none of them**, even if you don't agree with them all.

That's right, because they're all attached, every voting member has to vote yes or no to all of the attached bills.

Right about now, you're probably wondering, how can this be? None of this seems **right**. None of this seems **fair**. And, it definitely doesn't seem **democratic**.

You're right. The reason our Founding Fathers worked so hard to put **protections** into the Constitution is that they knew all about **human nature**. They knew that some people would serve the people they represent, but that others would be overcome with the power.

In a democracy where everyone does their job by paying attention, understanding issues, staying aware of politicians' actions, and using their voices, the **wayward politicians**, those who lose their way, wouldn't be a problem. Once people recognized that an official is not working for the common good, they could remove them from office or not re-elect them.

Unfortunately, modern day constituents aren't paying close attention and that creates **many problems**.

Wayward politicians, like sly foxes, put constituent issues at the bottom of the list.

They're making it hard for good lawmakers to do the work they were elected to do.

They're weakening our democracy and our place on the world stage as a leader.

Let's see what the **Tree of Democracy** looks like when we add the special interests, lobbies, riders, and darkness.

Imagine the trunk is our strong, sturdy government and the branches represent the three, co-equal branches of government. Now, we've added the **birds** to represent the **good special interests** who look to the tree for support. The **pests**, however, represent the **not-so-good special interests and lobbies** who damage the tree.

Finally, the moon and the night sky hide the **Riders**. The darkness of the night **obstructs vision** and the ability to see clearly. When riders are attached to a bill, usually at the last minute, the public doesn't see everything that's happening. **Spoiler Alert: Operating in darkness** is never a way to build trust.

First Amendment

Congress shall make
no law respecting an
establishment of religion,
or prohibiting the free exercise
thereof; or abridging the freedom
of speech, or of the press; or the
right of the people peaceably to
assemble, and to petition the
Government for a redress of grievances

At this point, you're probably thinking, this is seriously complicated and seems impossible to solve. With lobbies, special interests, campaign donations, riders and some power hungry politicians, how can the good politicians do the people's work?

Good news! We saved a really important concept for the perfect moment and that moment is here. It's called the **Free Press**. Living in a free country, we often take our freedoms for granted. One of democracy's most important freedoms is Freedom of the Press, conveniently located in the **1st Amendment**.

You've probably heard the word amendment many, many times and if you're like most people, you've probably never given it much thought. A Constitutional Amendment is actually **a correction, a revision, or an improvement to the original Constitution** that was approved in 1788. That means that since our Founding Fathers created this amazing document, it has had some changes.

The First Amendment states that Congress shall make no law respecting an establishment of religion, or prohibiting the free exercise thereof; or abridging the freedom of speech, or of the press; or the right of the people peaceably to assemble, and to petition the government for a redress of grievances.

That's a lot of freedoms packed into one amendment: freedom of religion, speech, press, assembly, and to petition the government.

Having an amendment approved is not an easy process. Two thirds of the House and Senate must approve the proposal and then three fourths of the states must approve it. **Since 1788, there have been 27 Amendments approved, six have been disapproved, and thousands that have simply been discussed.**

So how does the **First Amendment** help with the pitfalls of democracy?

That's easy, **Freedom of the Press** is often referred to as the **fourth branch or pillar** of government. That comparison is to help people understand its importance.

The media plays an important role in delivering information between the government and the people. Without the work of journalists, we would be unable to participate in our democracy. A free press provides people with the information needed to make decisions.

In America, the press is not only allowed to report on elected officials, they are expected to protect the public interest. Their work **shapes opinions, prompts actions**, and serves as **the people's watchdog**.

Why is protecting Freedom of the Press so important?

THE PEOPLE

Ensures citizens are aware and informed of issues and actions.

THE GOVERNMENT

Shines daylight on our elected and appointed officials.

It's time to make a change to our **Tree of Democracy**.

When we protect and value our free press, we remove the darkness and allow daylight to shine down. And much like darkness aids bad behavior, **daylight encourages good behavior**.

As citizens of a free country, we must rely upon a free press to share information and monitor the government. The information provided is the only way we, as voters and future voters, can participate and cast smart votes.

Hot Topics Surrounding the Press

24-HOUR NEWS CYCLES

When the first Colonial newspaper was printed in 1690, the colonists were excited. The British Governor, however, was not excited. There was a reason that all books and printed materials needed to have his permission. Those in power wanted **total control of the information** that the people could access. With no television or radio, newspapers were seen as a **form of disobedience**.

The best way for the government to control the people was to control the information. Of course, after the Revolution, that all changed and the free press became a necessary tool for citizens. But, only in recent years have we had so much news. Even in the 1970s, there were limited opportunities to receive the news of the day. With very few television stations and no internet, most people relied on the **evening news and daily newspapers**.

As technology exploded, the volume of news also exploded. Suddenly, there were hundreds of television stations, satellite radio stations, and the internet. With advancements in printing, printed media also exploded with more publications coming out more frequently. Blogs, which didn't exist before in the 1980s, have become the main source of news for many people, even though **many blogs are opinions**.

Today, news cycles run **24 hours a day, 7 days a week**. This constant bombardment of news has become a double-edged sword. On one side of the sword, it provides lots of opportunities for people to be informed. If you miss the evening news, you can turn to a news channel any time of day or night, or simply **look online**.

On the other side of the sword, many believe we now have too much news and rather than stay informed, people often tune it out. In addition, the non-stop news cycle and fierce competition means networks and news organizations must constantly search for news and exciting ways to present it.

FACT

The role of a free press and the honor and integrity of journalism require **objective coverage**. That means the journalists and reporters should **only report facts**. A real journalist never lets the reader or viewer know their true feelings. A journalist's goal is to provide you with facts and information.

OPINION

Commentators on the other hand, are not even journalists and many do not follow the same **journalistic standards**. They are simply providing their own **interpretation and opinions**. A commentator's goal is to shape and influence your opinion by using their opinions.

Where Did You Hear That?

Today, to fill the time and space, many organizations use opinion shows and writers in addition to news. It's up to the viewer/reader to know the difference, as well as the source of the information.

It's also smart to know about any **connections** an organization has with other groups or organizations. Some groups **disguise their opinions as facts** to influence how people think.

Suppose you're reading an article online and it supports the fact that doors should be ovals instead of rectangles. The article may present really strong reasons as to why ovals would make better doors. **But wait!** Before you become convinced, do some digging. **Who wrote the article? Who published it?**

Your research might uncover that the publisher of the article is the XYZ News Company. A little more digging might show that the company that owns XYZ News is, you guessed it, the Oval Door Company.

Aha!! That was not an objective piece of journalism. Instead it's an advertisement disguised as journalism. The bad news: they don't tell you they're **trying to trick you**. The good news: it only takes **a tiny amount of digging** to see if it's journalism.

The ironic thing is that they call this the **Communication Age**. And, it is. The problem is there's too much **useless, incorrect, and trivial** communication clogging up the airwaves and giving people **information fatigue**.

CHAPTER FOUR

Be an Amazing Citizen

That may sound easy, but it takes effort. Historically, Americans have had an **amazing zest for liberty and freedom** and have sacrificed a great deal to protect it. But, it's almost as if, once the Revolution ended, **interest faded**.

Why are so many people **uninterested** and **uninformed?** Why do so many Americans, who enjoy more freedoms than any country on the planet, take those **freedoms for granted**. With so many dictatorships in the world, why do so many Americans fail to exercise their hard-fought right to vote on **election day and beyond?**

Maybe people tune out because there are so many levels of government and paying close attention could feel like a full-time job.

Maybe it's because the *not-so-decent* politicians make things purposely complicated in hopes that people will get frustrated and tune out.

Maybe it's because voters watch politicians show up at diners, shake hands and kiss babies before the election. Everywhere you turn, they're there. But, once they get elected, you can barely get an intern to return an email.

They're all valid reasons. There are a lot of governments to monitor, things are very complicated, and people have been disappointed by their elected officials so often that they have become soured.

People often suggest that we **change how government operates.** They say we should do things like stop letting lobbyists and special interests donate so much money to candidates because it's like they're buying the votes they would like. Others say we should limit the length of the campaign season. A super long season requires more money and voters get campaign fatigue. That means they get so tired of seeing signs and watching commercials, that they don't pay attention. Some people think lawmakers should have the same type of term limit as the president—two terms.

So, why don't these things happen? **Think about it**. The people who would need to vote for these things, **lawmakers**, are the exact people who benefit from them. We cannot expect people who will **do almost anything to get elected** and then, if they do get elected, spend a great deal of their term **planning to get re-elected**, to make these kinds of changes.

Remember those words we mentioned before, **campaign finance reform?** Well, it's hard to believe this situation will somehow correct itself, especially after the **Citizens United** Supreme Court decision. Not sure what that is, keep reading.

There have been and still are definite **limits** as to how much a person, a group, or a company can **donate directly to a candidate's campaign**.

There are also things called **Political Action Committees**, or **PACs**. These are groups that are **not part of the campaign**, yet they support a candidate or an issue.

Once upon a time, there were **limits** on exactly how much money individuals and groups could donate as well as how they could use that money. But for decades there was a debate as to whether or not campaign contributions were **a form of free speech**. Remember Free Speech from the First Amendment? The **Citizen's United PAC** took the case to the United States Supreme Court, or SCOTUS, and argued that their First Amendment rights were being violated. In a 5-4 decision, the court agreed.

The decision stated that PACs must be **independent of the campaign** and **communication between the two is illegal**, but PACs could raise and spend as much money as they like. They could run ads and create commercials which **influence how people think**. Many people opposed the decision because, instead of limiting the amount of money spent during campaigns, it **removed the limits that could be spent if the money goes to a PAC**.

So, you're probably thinking... **wow, this is hopeless.**

The people who need to make the changes are the lawmakers, but **they benefit** from keeping things the same. Why on earth would they vote against things that help them stay in office? It's like telling a kid who has no bedtime to give himself a bedtime. **We all know that probably won't happen.**

What do we do? Remember that **equation** we discussed earlier.

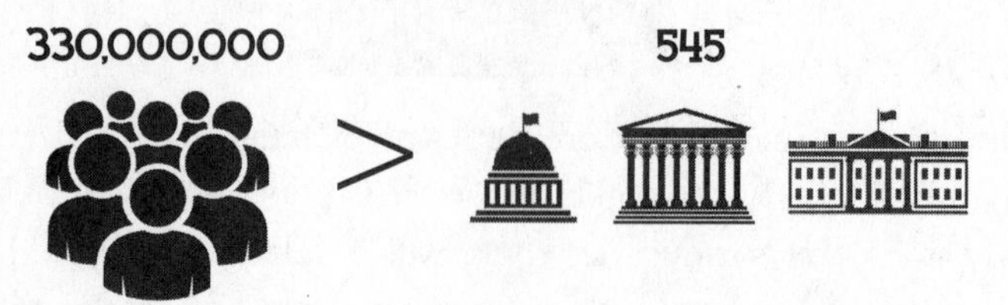

And, remember the **Tree of Democracy?** Not the first one, and not the one with moonlight, but the one with the sunlight of the free press. That tree reminds us that we must protect the sunlight provided by the First Amendment, **but that's not enough.**

Our youngest generation must become **Generation Lead** and must be ready and willing to lead the way, correcting mistakes of past generations. **You can do it.**

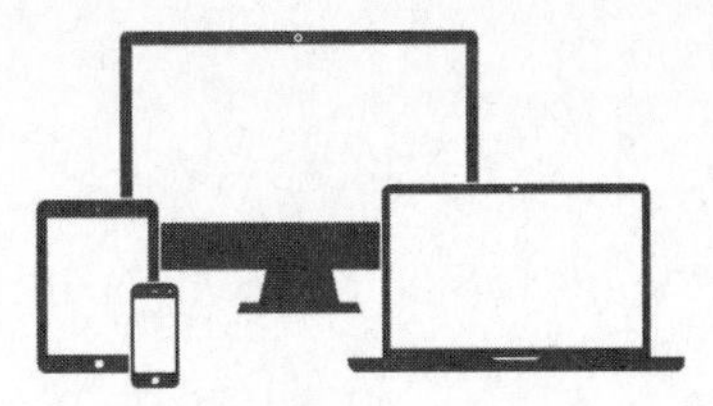

Never before has a generation had as much **access to real-time information**. Never before has a generation had such a unique opportunity to understand global issues. But, never before has a generation had **so many distractions**.

Yup, that's right. In the 1970s and the 1980s, kids were still using **encyclopedias** to find information. The amount of information in an encyclopedia was **very limited**. There was much less general knowledge about other countries and things that were going on in the world. And with a dozen or so television channels, no video games, no cell phones, no ipods or tablets, and no internet, there were **fewer distractions**.

Today's kids have what was **once unimaginable access to information**, but also the distractions of social media, games, thousands of channels, and non-stop communication. So, how does this generation train a government? That's easy. Our Founding Fathers provided the tools to get the job done. Just approach it **one step at a time!**

"What if we don't change at all… and something magical just happens?"

CHAPTER FIVE

How to Train Your Government

Make a Decision

That's right, step one is to make a decision that you want to train your government. They often say that if you're not part of the solution, you're part of the problem. This is where you have to decide if you want to be a **part of the solution**, knowing it won't always be easy.

This is where you have to summon your inner Paul Revere, your inner Susan B. Anthony, your inner Martin Luther King, and your inner Cesar Chavez.

If you don't know who some of those folks are, use one of your devices and Google their names. That's right, close the games and social media apps and read about the lives of some people who just may inspire you. Let those *smart* devices make *you* even **smarter**.

Take Small Steps

Once you make the decision to train your government, don't get carried away. Start with **very small steps**. Remember, this is a change and change isn't always easy.

Think about every adult who shared a New Years Resolution with you. Maybe they declared they would start a diet and exercise everyday, maybe they declared they would read five new books every month, maybe they declared they would drink more water. If you paid attention, you may have noticed a **strong effort in the beginning**. Unfortunately, when it comes to change, most people can't maintain that level of effort. They become disappointed and eventually quit.

Don't try to **sprint through a marathon**. The goal is for a lifelong change. **Learn from others' mistakes** and start with very small steps.

Take Strategic Steps

Small steps are important, but do you know what is just as important? **Strategic steps**. After you have decided to be a part of the solution, think long and hard about the best way to start. Maybe you will simply watch the news or read a few newspaper articles each day. Maybe you will google an issue that interests you and, using numerous websites, educate yourself and try to understand all sides. Maybe you'll talk to a variety of adults. Keep in mind, most people have a **definite point of view**, so their information will come from that perspective. It's best to find people from all points of view.

Becoming informed can be as easy or as hard as you make it. The old expression, **work smarter, not harder** applies here. This is not the time to count on luck. Take advantage of the internet and your devices to understand issues. Stop by a convenience store and pick up **a newspaper**. A lot of journalists go to a lot of trouble to bring you the information you need to stay informed. Plus, there's something very powerful about holding that newspaper in your hands.

Consider the Source

Whether you get your information from your sweet old granny, a newspaper, or a radio talk show, know the source. There is **often a very obvious bias**, a feeling for or against an issue, so **be observant**. When consuming news, be aware of the source and the source's point of view.

Avoid the headlines

Headlines are designed to grab your attention and they often **exaggerate** or **mislead** to get you to read the story. Don't be a headliner. Don't be that person who reads a headline or watches the first twenty seconds of a news show and then repeats parts of a story and makes up the rest. Remember, technology makes it **easy to be fooled**, but it's just as easy to find the truth if you really look.

Break the Cardinal Rule

My grandfather once told me about the cardinal rule. You may have never heard of this, but he said many people live by this rule: **never discuss politics and religion**. He said the reason is that people feel so strongly about their political points of view and their religion, that it **can only lead to arguments**.

We all agree that we disagree with this rule. Most wars and conflicts begin with differences in religion and politics. The cardinal rule shouldn't be "don't discuss religion and politics." It should be, **"don't be disrespectful when discussing religion and politics."** But discuss, discuss, discuss!

Let's face it, just knowing facts and information isn't enough. Appreciating that other people have different points of view and understanding why they feel the way they do won't just make you a better citizen, it will make you a better person. Remember, knowledge is power, and in this global community, the more you know, the better! Just keep it respectful.

Take Positions, NOT SELFIES

Okay, you might want to **have a seat for this one**. By this point you should have a **position**, or at least some thoughts, on various issues. If you feel passionately about a topic, know your topic inside and out, and then take a position.

But, here's the dreaded fine print: as you mature, as you enjoy more experiences, as you meet more people, as you learn more, something unexpected may happen. **Your positions may change**.

Yup, what you believe today may change tomorrow. That's okay, as long as you always base your positions on facts and not headlines or sketchy sources.

This is also why its important to be able to **defend a position**, respectfully, but to never look down on others. You never know what the future holds, so don't paint yourself into a corner.

If, however, you don't know enough about a topic, it's not only acceptable, but it's wise to say you don't know enough to take a position. What isn't wise is to rely on headlines or conversations with others without fact-checking the information.

Party Time

So, you live in a democracy that is generally considered a **two-party system** and those two parties are the **Democrats** and the **Republicans**. You should know that there are other parties, too, even though you may have never heard of them. Ironically, the most significant one isn't even a party. It's simply called being an **Independent**. As an Independent voter, you vote for candidates and issues, instead of every candidate who represents your party.

Each party, whether it's one of the major two, or one of the many smaller parties, has a platform which showcases their beliefs.

You don't have to commit to a party because it's the party your family supports and you don't have to commit because everyone else does. What you do have to do is educate yourself.

Before you pick a party, **do your homework**. Some parties are still affiliated with ideals they **used to support**, but no longer actually support. And, yes, that's super easy to check.

Some parties have evolved and made changes that even members of the party don't know about. Some elected party members' votes don't reflect the platform of the party. Also super easy to check.

As you learn about each party, you may find that your ideas line up pretty close with one party. **But be prepared**. You may also find that some of your ideas line up with one party, while some line up with another party.

That's okay, and basically how independent voters were born. They don't strictly vote for a party, but for candidates and their positions on issues. Some are independents who lean toward a party, but they aren't locked in. Just remember, **you have options!**

We the People

Know Your Rights

As we discussed earlier, you are very lucky to live in a country that was founded upon one of the most important documents ever written: **The Constitution**.

The Constitution is the **Law of the Land** and it's a very **strategic document**. Our Founding Fathers knew that a government of the people was susceptible to **tyranny**, which is a very old word for people who want to use the government for their own benefit. They worked very hard to make sure the government could withstand attempts of tyranny with three co-equal branches and those **checks and balances**.

What are checks and balances? A system that prevents any one branch from becoming too powerful. The Executive Branch can veto bills from the Legislative Branch, but the Legislative Branch, with enough votes, can override the veto. Members of the Supreme Court are appointed for life by the president and approved by Congress. But the Supreme Court can declare Congress's laws unconstitutional.

Now, you may be wondering how a document created over 200 years ago could still be **relevant**. When they wrote it, there were no cars, telephones, airplanes, or public schools as we know them today. They didn't even have refrigerators. How could those laws from the past still apply today?

The Constitution was written to allow for those differences and it has changed over the years to reflect changes in thought or daily life. By using amendments, Congress and the people can make necessary adjustments.

In 1869, the Fifteenth Amendment granted African American men the right to vote. Until 1920, women were still not allowed to vote. It wasn't until August 18, 1920 that the Nineteenth Amendment gave women the right to vote. Up until then, that right was reserved only for men.

One important step in being a great citizen and training your government is understanding the laws of the land. Now, we know what you're thinking, the Constitution looks a little hard to read. **And that's true**. But have no fear, there are books and websites that translate it to modern, **everyday language with explanations**. Some even use great pictures!

You may also be interested in the **Twenty-sixth Amendment**, approved in 1971, which lowered the minimum age to vote from 21 years old to 18 years old. That means that you can cast your **first vote at 18 years old**.

This is very important as there are countries where no elections are ever held. That's right, **some countries have no elections**, some try to appear to hold fair and free elections even though there is only one candidate, and some have elections but make it almost impossible for many people to vote. You're lucky. Make it a point to **never miss an election**, whether it's for President of the United States or town dog catcher, **remember to vote**.

Use Your Voice

By now, you know how to find accurate information, you know all about parties, and you know the value of respectful debate, especially when it's about politics and religion. That's great! Now, you have to learn how to **use your voice**. First, let's see what some **pretty wise voices** had to say about the importance of that voice.

"Speak softly, but carry a big stick."
—*Theodore Roosevelt*

This isn't actually about carrying a stick, it's about knowing the issue and being respectful, but knowing when to be tough. The stick represents your power.

"Above all, tell the truth."
—*Grover Cleveland*

This one is pretty self-explanatory.

"You can never get all of the facts from just one newspaper, and unless you have all the facts, you cannot make proper judgements about what is going on."
—Harry S. Truman

This means you should always use multiple sources and understand different points of view.

"Liberty without learning is always in peril, and learning without liberty is always in vain."
—John F. Kennedy

"Let us not forget that government is ourselves and not an alien power over us. The ultimate rulers of our democracy are not a President, senators and congressmen and government officials, but the voters of this country."
—Franklin D. Roosevelt

"Change will not come if we wait for some other person or some other time. We are the ones we've been waiting for. We are the change that we seek."
—Barack Obama

As you can see, democracy is a **participatory form of government** which means we all must participate in order for it to be its best. All too often, people proudly declare that they don't follow politics. Some offer **excuses**, some say they don't care, some don't believe their opinion matters. Here are some of the most common excuses from real people that we spoke with:

> "Nobody listens anyway. They pretend to listen and then they just do whatever helps them and their own families."
>
> "You can't fight City Hall. People always try, but in the end, the people with power and authority always win."
>
> "I don't have time. I have kids, a job, bills, and older parents I take care of."
>
> "Every time I support a candidate, they end up lying or breaking their promises. When I call the office, I can never speak with my representative."
>
> "I am so sick of hearing them attack their opponents and I'm really tired of hearing their commercials over and over. It never ends."

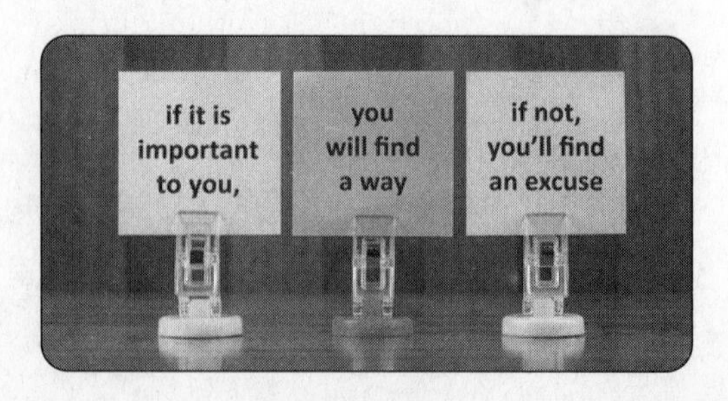

As members of the next generation, make it your job to do everything possible to **preserve our democracy**. That means using your well-informed voice. Need suggestions? Look no further:

Call your elected or government officials to ask questions or to comment on current events.

Send a letter or an e-mail to your elected or government officials presenting your point of view.

Make an appointment to meet your elected or government officials. Share your thoughts and any concerns. Arrive prepared.

Discuss current events with your family and friends. Be prepared, some may only read headlines or watch one network. You'll be able to tell.

Attend meetings to see how government actually works and speak during the public portion.

Write a compelling letter to the editor of your local newspaper about a current event that you feel strongly about.

As soon as you turn 18 years old, register and vote in your first election. Then vote in every election after that. And, remind others to vote.

The most important part of using your voice will shock you. It has nothing to do with speaking, meeting, writing, or calling. In fact, the thing that most prepares you for using your voice is **listening**.

Remember, you don't learn from speaking, you learn from listening. You may not agree with what others say, but there are **always things you can learn**.

Don't avoid speaking to people who have different points of view. **Big mistake!** It's almost impossible to learn from someone who feels just like you do.

When you do speak to someone who has a different point of view, there's never a reason for the discussion to get heated. If you feel that the person you're speaking to is getting angry, **respectfully end the conversation**.

Agree to disagree. The goal of a discussion or debate with someone who has a different point of view shouldn't be convincing the other person to think like you do. Most of the time that won't happen. Be happy to simply give the other person something a little different to consider.

When you do speak, however, **follow these rules:**

When you use your voice, **stay calm**. Depending upon the topic, people can often get very emotional. It's hard to sound truly intelligent if you let **emotions get in the way**.

Stick to the topic. Sometimes, when people feel they are losing a debate, they start veering off topic. If you do this, it's a sign that you aren't prepared or well-versed about the issue.

Don't interrupt. Yup, that one sounds simple, but guess what? As soon as someone gets into a conversation they are passionate about, **manners often go out the window**. Force yourself to listen to the other person, waiting for pauses before speaking.

Never, under any circumstances, **make fun of someone** or their opinion. Not only is it mean, **you WILL lose your credibility**. Remember, you don't have to agree, but you do have to be respectful.

You may hear terms like **fake news**, **bias**, and **alternative facts**. It's important, as a constituent and future voter, that you understand what these terms mean.

Fake news implies that a news organization has **purposely lied**. While it's true that mistakes can be made, very rarely are they made on purpose. And, when they are made, they are retracted.

The facts, however, show that what some people call fake news are really stories that are **unflattering**. As a consumer of news, you must be able to tell the difference between **bias** and fake news.

Bias is when a story is told from a specific point of view, instead of objectively. Some organizations tell all of their stories through bias. Fake news, however, is usually reserved for tabloid magazines near the grocery store cash registers. Your best bet is to fact check and use multiple sources and common sense.

As for **Alternative Facts**: facts are facts. Facts are true. Alternative facts are **lies**. Period.

CHAPTER SIX

Rules for Your Representatives

In a government that is by the people, for the people, and of the people, the people have tremendous power… **when they use it.** The key words: **when they use it.** For quite some time, though, *the people* haven't been paying attention. When they do pay attention, *the people* can do amazing things. Remember, **we the people outnumber the elected officials.** Look at the numbers.

	Total People	Total People in Three Branches
United States	330,000,000	545
New Jersey	9,000,000	128
California	39,000,000	128
Connecticut	3,500,000	195
Texas	28,000,000	191
Pennsylvania	13,000,000	261

What's up with Washington DC?

Washington DC is **not** one of the 50 states, but it is our nation's capital. Congress established the federal district from land belonging to Maryland and Virginia in 1790. Basically, our Founding Fathers worried that if the capital was a state, members of the government would **treat it differently.** They felt so strongly about it, that it's in the Constitution: **Article I, Section 8, Clause 17.**

But wait! If Washington DC isn't a state, what does that mean? For starters, the residents of WDC aren't thrilled about the situation. They have no governor or senators, and its one representative has no vote in the House. It wasn't until 1961 that the 23rd Amendment granted the District **three electoral college votes,** equal to the smallest state. So residents can vote for President, their one Representative, Mayor, and Council, but **their member of the House of Representatives cannot vote.**

It's not because they don't have enough people to become a state as they have **more people** than some states. And it's not because they don't pay taxes, they actually **pay more** than every other state. Unless they become a state however, the situation will stay the same.

If you ever have a chance to visit Washington DC, check out their license plates:

Taxation without Representation!

A Deal They Can't Refuse

For so long, voters have had enormous power, but didn't realize how powerful they actually were. Now, it's time to start **responsibly wielding power** and to **accept the responsibilities and the rights of citizenship**. And, it's time to recognize that our elected, appointed, and government officials **work for us** and should support our best interests.

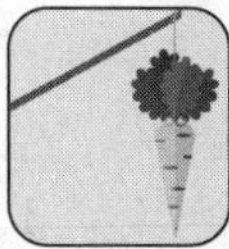

Perhaps it's time to offer them a deal they can't refuse. Training the government requires **Knowing what motivates them** and what makes them listen. We have to figure out exactly what we want and what we'll offer. The offer part is easy, **voters can offer their vote**.

Politicians also need help to **spread their message**, whether it's about getting elected or supporting their bills, **participation is another motivator**. Whether it's knocking on doors, or making phone calls, they can always use volunteers.

And of course, we know that **they need campaign donations** to continue to run for re-election. So how we donate and how the groups we belong to donate, can be a motivator.

Social Media For The Greater Good

Serving as an elected, appointed, or government official is an amazing honor. The people who hold those positions, however, should be **held to a higher standard**. As a future voter, you should decide what you will expect from the people you elect.

If you were to speak to all of the people who complain about the government, you would get a lot of **suggestions**. Everyone has their own ideas about what would make government better. Most of those ideas, however, are **partisan**, meaning they support one party's ideas, either Democrat or Republican. But, what if you forgot about the issue of party and simply **focused on behavior?** What if every voter could use a list of behaviors to measure their candidates?

Now, you probably have some questions. How exactly would you let candidates know about **The List?** How would you know if they were following the suggestions on the list? What could voters do if candidates ignored the list?

Those are great questions. The **technology** that allows people to share silly things like what they had for breakfast can also be used **for important things**. What if social media was used for the **greater good?** What if, rather than spending countless hours liking things and posting selfies, people **collectively kept tabs on elected officials** and shared that information? What if the absolute longest online streaks were for sharing political information? Sounds like a lot of work? It wouldn't feel like a full-time job if **the work was split between a few hundred million people!**

But, there's still that last question; what could voters do when some candidates violated The List? That's easy. **Don't give them your very valuable vote**. And if, sadly, there are no candidates that follow the list, once elected, **follow the candidate**. Use your social media to share what they're doing. Like the Free Press, **shine your own daylight**.

The Possibilities

Suppose you created a document called **The List** and it contained those suggestions and let all candidates know that you would only consider voting for those that respected the list. And what if you weren't the only person using that list? What if **so many voters used the list** that it changed the way politics operated and improved the work of the government?

What if politics became something that everyone, **even kids**, monitored? And what if politics went from being a topic to be avoided to a topic that was **discussed as frequently as the weather?** What if politicians continued to visit the diners and fairs, even after elections? **What if people started feeling good about government?**

The List

We the people take a government by the people, for the people, and of the people seriously. We also take our collective right to vote seriously. For that reason, we are revising our criteria for candidates, using The List.

In order for a voter to consider casting a vote for you, the following criteria must be met. Those who cannot meet the criteria will not receive our votes or support.

1. **Honesty** *— when it comes to telling the truth, we expect no more from you than that which is expected of small children. Tell the truth. All of the time. This includes avoiding lies of omission. Don't try to be cute or clever and if you don't know the answer, "I'm not sure," is completely acceptable. If you choose to lie, because lying is a choice, your lies will be shared with all voters and violates The List.* **For clarification, this is a biggie.**

2. **Transparency** *— there should be no secret meetings or deals. Transparent means we should be able to see what's happening. Failure to behave in a transparent manner leads people to believe you are up to no good. If you have nothing to hide, this shouldn't be a problem.* **Also a biggie.**

3. **Communication** *— we all know that candidates are easy to find during the campaign season, but will you be accessible once you are elected? To be considered for a vote, candidates must agree to be available to respond to the needs of those you're elected to serve.*

4. **Negativity** *— rather than attack your opponent's personal life and professional record, we, the voters, prefer you abide by the typical kindergarten rule of remaining quiet if you have nothing nice to say. Tell us your positives.*

5. **Advertisements** *— your advertisements should be suitable for all viewers, honest, and transparent. They also should focus on your qualifications or accomplishments and shouldn't run day and night. We need a break.*

Signed,
The People

Campaign Idea from Around the World

In the United States, in 2012, only **53.6%** of registered voters showed up at the polls and cast a vote in the presidential election. That's just **a little more than half** of all of the citizens who could have and should have voted. In case you're thinking that's just human nature, **think again**. Then use that smart phone or tablet to find out what's happening around the world. According to Business Insider:

In **Switzerland**, all voters receive a ballot by mail ahead of election day. Anyone can **vote by mail** for any reason.

In **Sweden**, people are **automatically** registered to vote.

Countries like **Finland**, **Iceland**, **Luxembourg**, and **New Zealand** hold elections on **Saturday/Sunday** to maximize turnout.

India, has made election day a **national holiday** that grants public and private workers the day off.

Belgium isn't the only country where voting is **mandatory**, there are roughly two dozen in total, and they have the highest voter turnout.

Australia lets people **vote anywhere**, at any location, in their state.

In a country built on democracy, ask yourself if we are doing everything we can do to increase voter participation.